A MAN ABOVE
REPROACH

A MAN ABOVE REPROACH

EVELYN PRYCE

The characters and events portrayed in this book are fictitious. Any similarity to real persons, living or dead, is coincidental and not intended by the author.

Text copyright © 2013 Kristin K. Ross

Published by Montlake Romance
P.O. Box 400818 Las Vegas, NV 89140
ISBN-13: 9781477848173
ISBN-10: 1477848177

Library of Congress Control Number: 2013909203

To my husband, Stephen M. Foland, a rare and true man above reproach.

CHAPTER ONE

ENGLAND, 1832

The table shook, rattling the gentlemen's glasses. The culprit of the minor earthquake was Elias Addison, the newly minted and reluctant Duke of Lennox, who was having trouble fulfilling his friend's request to "relax and try to be merry." Nicholas had dragged him to the Sleeping Dove, but Elias could not stop the restless shuffling of his feet as worries and lists ran through his mind.

"Are you nervous, Lennox?"

Elias turned his eyes to Lord Nicholas Thackeray, the heir presumptive to the Marquess of Bristol and his closest friend. Since attending school together, they had been inseparable, for better or worse. Elias often thought Nicholas encouraged him into too many excessive debauches, though his friend would insist they were "adventures." Once Elias had inherited the title, he had become a difficult man to wrest from his estate. His mood was black and his conversation no better. He thought constantly about the responsibilities that had been dumped into his lap, debts and all. It was not as if he were ill-prepared, but he had half-expected his father to live forever. Between funeral arrangements, creditors, and the great disorganized volume of paper in his father's study, Elias found his taste for pleasures distinctly dulled. His listlessness was the reason that Nicholas had insisted he accompany him to the club in Covent Garden, known for its mysterious back rooms.

"I guarantee we will find distraction here," Nicholas continued, without waiting for an answer to his question. "The servants and accounting books at Ashworth will still be waiting for you in the morning, but they will disappear from your mind at the first sight of the women here, old boy."

Old boy, indeed, Elias thought to himself. He was thirty-one, and his mother did not hesitate to remind him that she would be more than willing to take up residence at the dowager house if it meant that he married. The question of an heir was even more pressing now that he possessed the Lennox title. Yet he just could not imagine a lifetime with any of the simpering misses he was forced to dance with at every exhausting ball, those debutantes with one eye on his fortune and the other on the word "duchess." Did they care that he was a deft hand at the pianoforte and rather enjoyed the way the light leaked out of the windows in his library every evening? Did they care that before his father died, he had been considering leaving court for good to take up a professorship? Did they care that he hated shooting, but he did it anyway, merely because it was considered a gentlemanly activity? Did they care that he never let his valet tie his cravat, as a secret point of pride?

He was quite sure they did not.

Nicholas snapped him out of reverie by standing and handing him a plain black half-face mask as if it were a secret document. Men all around were slipping away, toward a hallway in the back of the tavern, the very one Nicholas was sneaking glances toward in an expectant fervor.

"You will need to put on the mask once we reach that hallway; Mother Superior does not allow gentlemen to show their faces. Something to be said about efforts made to keep the peers' predilections private." He grinned, pleased with his alliteration.

"It seems ridiculous to me," Elias said, looking down at the mask, "since you can tell who is who, in any case."

"Play along, Elias." Nicholas sounded exasperated, and that finally pulled a tiny smile onto Elias's face. It was amusing when Nicholas called him by his Christian name in public and he knew it was

2

employed to make a point. He followed along behind his friend, hoping the Sleeping Dove at least had some good brandy.

Once in the hallway, he pulled the mask over his head, mussing his hair even further than it already had been. He had let it grow too long, he admitted, but it was not yet disrespectable. Now that he was the duke, no one would dare tell him that he was wrong. It had become almost a game to him, to test the boundaries. Breaking little society rules was the only joy he had in recent memory.

They joined the line in the cramped hallway. The Sleeping Dove had become a popular attraction. Nicholas had mentioned earlier that the gossips claimed Mother Superior's den was a breeding ground for the best ladybirds, some of whom eventually became high-priced mistresses. Not that Elias was looking for a mistress. He thought his peers did despicable deeds simply out of abundance and boredom. His father had been such a man. They let their estates run into ruin while they occupied themselves in the pursuits of momentary satisfaction. They strained against the strict rules of society, which made no allowance for their appetites, and they needed places such as this where the patronesses and wives did not exist. There was a part of Elias that understood this intimately and another part that felt disgust. The latter part began to grow upon looking at his father's bookkeeping and wondering where a large chunk of his and his sister's inheritance had gone.

A cloud of noxious perfume washed over him as a buxom woman wove her way to the front of the line.

"That is Mother Superior," Nicholas whispered like a conspirator. "She's the one who has charge of all of the girls. If she likes you, you will want for nothing. But of course, you are a duke now, and everyone likes you."

Elias snorted through the preposterous mask and tried in vain to smooth his hair. Strands of it were tangled in the string of the mask now, threatening to knot. The damned thing worsened his derisive expression, instead of obscuring it.

"I am having second thoughts about this, Thackeray."

"Nonsense." Nicholas was now so excited that he was barely paying attention to Elias, bouncing up and down on his heels, verging on the idiotic. "Believe me. You will be grateful once we're inside. Have I ever steered you wrong before?"

"Yes. Indeed you have."

A murmur of anticipation went through the line of men as the doors to the back room opened. A mix of alcohol and sweat hit Elias's nostrils, which flared in protest. He would have to slip out of the brothel undetected to avoid getting an earful from Nicholas. That was not a fate he would enjoy—Nicholas was impossible to argue with. It would be better to just stay for at least a quarter hour and have a drink. Ladies were not very high on his list of priorities, but the liquor would be appreciated.

Mother Superior appraised Elias as he tried to slip unobtrusively through the doors. She put an arm across the entrance with a saucy flair. The madam of the brothel bore every resemblance to a dishrag: flat, limp hair and a soiled gingham apron over a muslin dress past its prime. She even looked a bit damp. Her shrewd green eyes appraised them as she blocked the door. Elias would have put her age at sixty, but her cracked makeup was trying to hide the truth.

"You're new," she purred. "A friend of yours, Nicholas?"

Elias felt his nose wrinkle at the informal way she addressed Nicholas. Then again, Nicholas was a regular visitor and he must have given her permission.

"Yes, not that it is your concern," Elias replied, pressing his lips together. He had been told he had a cruel mouth, which he used to his advantage when he could. He didn't care if the madam knew his identity; he didn't plan on doing anything untoward and he wanted this woman to know exactly who she was dealing with. "The Duke of Lennox."

"Your Grace," she said, dipping into a deep curtsy that better displayed her bosom. "Forgive me. Welcome. I will make sure you have first choice of the company of our fine ladies this evening."

He bowed slightly in acknowledgement but felt sickened by both the groveling and the swelling of her chest, barely kept in place by her gown. Overripe. He began counting the minutes before he could leave unnoticed. His eyes searched the crowd for Nicholas, who had already deserted him for gentler company. Elias could see him across the room, bantering with a scantily clad beauty in all red. Her elaborate mask was covered in feathers and beads of the same color.

"They call her Crimson and you can see why," Mother Superior said from over his shoulder, her eyes having followed his. "Your friend has taken quite a fancy to her over the past few weeks."

Elias held back a rude grunt. He managed to turn it into a polite sound that was a mix of disinterest and civility.

"Shall we get you a drink, Your Grace?"

He could see her thought process: get them in, get them drunk, get them bedded. No matter. Elias's resolve was legendary—though his family would call it stubbornness—and he needed to get a little foxed. He would keep his head about him. A few drinks, then back home by hired carriage. He certainly hadn't brought the carriage with his family crest into this establishment. Elias followed Mother Superior with resignation, recognizing members of the House of Lords and pillars of the church community among the crowd. As he'd suspected, the masks were wholly ineffective.

He curled his hand around the glass of brandy, which did not approach the quality of the bottle on his desk at Ashworth Hall. He longed for his beautiful mahogany desk, his sequestered room where he could tell his butler to not let anyone in, where there was not a constant chatter of people who cared only about rutting.

From behind him, tentative and soft notes issued from a piano. The player was being very courteous, playing a light, frothy tune that provided atmosphere without intruding on the merriment. It was mildly humorous to him, this gent playing in a whorehouse. What an odd employment that must be; the stories he must have to tell. Elias turned to see the make of the man, but ended up choking on his surprise.

"Ah, Lennox," Nicholas chuckled, appearing at his shoulder. "Trust you to fix on the only lady not for sale."

Elias's eyes tried to take in the full sight of her, seated on the bench with impossibly upright stature, compared to the other slumped womanly forms painted across the room. She wore an elaborate mask, beaded and feathered, that covered every bit of her face save her eyes and lips. Brown hair was piled high on her head, pinned to expose an elegant neck supporting her enticing collarbone. The décolletage on her gown was more conservative than he expected in a brothel. It dipped low enough to entice, but it was not anything beyond what was à la mode in the grand ballrooms of London. The skirt, however, was far beyond propriety, angled high in the front to expose legs that tested his sanity, wrapped around the bench and clad in bright-blue silk stockings.

"Lennox?" Nicholas still stood waiting for an answer to words that had disappeared into the thick air, unheard. Elias took a drink before speaking. He croaked through a twinge of pain in his throat, having swallowed harder than he intended.

"Yes?"

"I asked if you wanted to know her story, but I wager you do. That is the chit they call the Bawdy Bluestocking. Regulars call her BB. It is said that she's a courtesan, but I have not met the man that has kept her. Some say she's a society lady moonlighting here as a voyeur, to escape her loveless marriage, but I have looked her straight in the face and those eyes do not exist in our circles. Plays piano all night, and well. You can talk to her, but she charges for her time, and she does not do private audiences. Elias? Are you even listening to me?"

Elias knew that Nicholas's itinerant blue eyes were wide, but he didn't see them. He was already on his way to the corner.

He placed a few shillings on the piano.

"A conversation, madam?"

It was then that Elias Addison, the grave and stoic Duke of Lennox who always had a plan, realized he had no idea what he was doing.

◆   ◆   ◆

Josephine looked at the money, heard the voice she did not recognize, and then looked up to the regal man with his thin-fingered hand resting casually on the surface of her piano. It was a hand that had never done a day of manual labor. She could tell just by the cut of his jacket and the way he stood that he was a duke. She could just tell. She hated talking to these privileged men who acted as if they owned everything they surveyed.

"Of course, Your Grace," she nodded.

He quirked a brow. "Are we acquainted?"

"No, indeed, except that we are now. They call me BB around here, though I don't particularly fancy it."

She fancied nothing about the place, in point of fact, but it was a necessity. Contrary to the wild stories the men in the Sleeping Dove had concocted to make her a myth, her story was not so dramatic or unusual. Josephine Grant was a woman of modest monetary means and fewer connections. When her father left this world, all she got was the little bookshop he owned and with it all of his debtors. There was enough money coming in only to keep it afloat and to allow her to have one employee. Playing piano at the Dove was supposed to supplement her income, but when she learned of the true horrors there, it had become something more. That part, she supposed, was unusual.

"What would you prefer to be called?" the duke said, splitting her reverie.

"You needn't call me anything to converse. You and I are the only ones talking, we know to whom our address is directed." She hit a few notes, worried about the discordant value in them. The piano needed repair, but Mother Superior would not hear of it.

"Your instrument needs tuning."

"I doubt yours does," she said with a saucy smile. This was what most men who approached her wanted. Banter and innuendo to prime them to choose a woman among the girls Mother had plucked from the streets.

He sat down on the bench next to her. She really should not have allowed him; she did not allow that. The velvet of his jacket made her side overwarm. Of course, it was just the fabric. The expensive fabric that could probably pay a fair chunk of what her father owed to the barrister who was now threatening to take away the only thing she really owned, her beloved bookstore.

"Of course not. I keep my piano in the best possible condition. I play nightly and I can hear the slightest change in key. It would irritate me to no end to play this beast," he remarked.

There was no teasing in his tone. Josephine looked at him full-on. He had a dangerous face, not traditionally handsome, but one that invited further study. In fact, she found it hard to look away from the odd planes that existed there. The swoop of his cheekbones vanished into his mask, leaving half-moons in the shadows it created. She looked away, so as to keep her mind on the dialogue and not appear to be staring.

"With another seasoned player present, I hope I do not disappoint. Most of the time, I assume no one is listening."

He glanced around the room with a judgmental eye.

"I suspect you are correct on that count." He paused, seeming to realize he was being rude. "But it improves the ambience."

"True enough. It keeps the women's spirits up at least, they tell me. That alone keeps me here." Josie had no idea why she told him that, it was far too personal. She did not know what else to say, so she said what she was actually thinking. His strange, cold brown eyes and blank tone did not equate with the coarse language that was expected from men who put money on the table.

"Just that?"

"And money, of course." She smiled in what she hoped was a light-hearted manner. "Surely you do not think the bits o' muslin you see around you are here for their own entertainment?"

"I appreciate your candor." He put his fingers on the piano and tinkled out an airy melody. "Is that what they pay you for?"

"I would not say this tête-à-tête is representative of what I normally do."

"Which is?"

"Exactly what did you expect for mere shillings, Your Grace?"

His enigmatic manner was unsettling. The last thing she wanted was anyone nosing around asking questions. Josephine would rather keep a low profile and stay as much away from Mother Superior as possible.

"If you would call me Elias, I would call it even."

Those lips that might be unkind in another expression were devastating in a smile.

"That would be highly improper."

He chuckled. "And you are the height of propriety, Blue?"

Damned if that was not charming. This stoic peer and his unexpected nickname put a chink in her defenses. She would give him what he paid for, she decided.

"I think I will play some Thomas Moore for you later, Elias, while you drink your fill and find your lady. I wish you luck."

He bowed his head to her, his eyes capturing hers. The use of his name sparked something behind his mahogany orbs, the color lit with a roguish glow.

"I have found my lady, but I have yet to drink my fill." He gestured to the remains of his glass, the dark liquid swishing like nausea in the bottom. "This is swill, you know."

"Mother does not like to spend money frivolously."

"Good brandy is never frivolous." He put two pounds on the piano. "At least your madam did not charge me for it. It gives me leave to spend my money elsewhere."

"You are being far too extravagant."

"How much will buy your exclusive company for the evening?"

"I am sure you have been informed that this is not an option."

"I am not asking to share your bed," he said curtly. "I am asking for the freedom to speak with you whenever I wish."

"I must play," she squeaked. She hadn't meant to squeak. She was not one who made a habit of squeaking.

"Between songs. On breaks. How much?"

These dukes, these peers, they thought they could purchase whatever they wanted. It must have been the whiff of money, because there was Mother Superior, grinning.

"I would say a total of ten pounds, including what you've already spent, is a fair amount and I'll be sure that no other gentleman speaks with her this evening." She grinned so widely that her missing back teeth were on display.

"Mother . . ." Josephine started.

"Hush, BB, His Grace has been quite generous." The subtext of her sentence was that she would be taking a significant cut of that money. If many different men talked to Josephine over a course of an evening, it was easier for her to hide how much she had actually made.

As Mother Superior led the duke away for another drink—she would probably break into the better stash, now—Josephine bent down to her keys again. There was nothing to be done but to play.

❖   ❖   ❖

"You did what?" Nicholas said with disbelief, his crimson girl hanging happily on his arm. He and the lass must have been in their cups for some time now, as they clung to each other, tipsy.

"I gave her ten pounds to buy the whole of Blue's evening conversation."

"You mean the Bawdy Bluestocking?" Crimson piped in. Elias had found out Crimson's real name was Sally—she and Thackeray had reached a point in their arrangement where it felt silly for him to call her by only a color.

"She's a grand friend of mine," Sally went on. "Bit too serious sometimes, but you seem a bit serious, Your Grace." She grinned in a fetching way, and Elias could see how she had won Nicholas's admiration. She was another anomaly in this place—a truly beautiful girl among many tired and ruined women. She shone; stood out. Sally had a fetching, heart-shaped face and wide emerald eyes that stayed mainly focused on Nicholas. They matched each other well, Elias thought, her wavy brown hair just a touch lighter than the black of Nicholas's. He was about a head taller than her, making it easy for him to plant an affectionate kiss on her crown.

"Sally," Nicholas admonished, "Lennox has recently been through quite a lot."

"No, no," Elias said, taking another drink. The second brandy was much better, he noticed, and the amount more charitable. "She is right. I am a bit serious."

Nicholas squeezed her arm with affection. "You have gotten him to admit what I have been trying to for countless years."

Elias glanced over to the piano, where a radiant tune had begun to issue, blending as if it were written to be a line under the ever more raucous crowd. He did not recognize the composition, so he assumed it was original. This woman was actually going to the trouble of composing for this nanny house? She could not possibly be paid enough for that. The tune, even when off-key, was like a pair of creamy, powdered arms wrapped around the whole room. Blue's fingers danced across the keys evenly because they knew the way. Her eyes were closed. She was not there.

"He's staring," Sally whispered to Nicholas.

"He never stopped staring, love," Nicholas laughed. "Not since he saw her."

"She is no ordinary player," Elias said, ignoring their mockery. "She was classically trained somewhere and from a young age at that."

"I believe that is only one of her apparent gifts under your observation," Nicholas smirked.

Elias shot him a look and Sally giggled.

"She wouldn't mind your notice," she said. "The girls of the Dove are not uppity at all."

"Obviously not," Elias muttered. He wanted to keep his piano girl apart from the Cyprians swarming around him. He had not lied to her; he did not plan on taking her to bed. He was not going to try to seduce her. Their brief dialogue had distracted him enough to make him stay—he had underestimated the value of an intelligent woman's charming conversation. He could forget for a moment that his father had let the tenants near the country estate run wild and that he needed to plan for his sister's London debut. All that existed was that feathered mask and the full lips that lived under it. He hoped that she could talk while playing. Perhaps they could duet.

He was letting his idle fantasies get the best of him. A duke could not play piano in a bordello. Ridiculous.

His brandy had been refilled and he had not noticed. Nicholas was smiling in his direction.

"I told you time stops in this place," he said.

"Your friend is smitten!" Sally exclaimed, clapping her hands together with delight.

"Not smitten," Elias corrected. "Intrigued."

"Lennox would never stoop so low as to be smitten," Nicholas grinned. "Just ask any of the esteemed patronesses. He is impenetrable." He nuzzled against the girl's cheek contentedly. "They call him the Uncatchable. You should tell the bluestocking that tidbit."

"Your gentleman exaggerates," Elias corrected. "I just have high standards and none of the misses pushed in front of me at London balls have managed to meet them."

"BB's the classiest gal I've ever met. Always reading. Nice to everyone, doesn't matter their station in life. She helps the girls that Mother . . ." Sally cut off, her eyes darting away. "Never mind that, but she's almost an angel, Your Grace."

Mother Superior must have had a psychic sense about the mention of her name, because she glided into their circle, skirts swirling around her like a rough ocean that would make one seasick. She gave Sally a look of disapproval.

"My dear Crimson, I do hope you're not boring the gentlemen with chitchat. I have a room reserved for you and Lord Thackeray."

"Soon enough," Nicholas said, a bit snippily. "We are enjoying ourselves out here for the time being."

"Crimson does not get compensated for conversation," Mother purred, "but perhaps I should reconsider that agreement."

"Excuse me?"

Elias could see Thackeray's temper rising, so he stepped forward.

"I will not be offended. You two make use of the fine room that is waiting for you, whether it is for discussion or something more. I should get my pounds' worth of the bluestocking, at any rate."

"A gentleman who respects the rules," the madam smiled, too feline.

"It works both ways. Keep my glass filled and your nose well away from the piano."

He stood straighter, knowing that his height was rather imposing when he directed it accordingly. He turned before he could see her reaction, but could tell from Nicholas's smile that the remark had hit home.

"Good evening, Nicholas." He bowed in his best courtly manner and then kissed Sally's hand. "It was a pleasure to have made your acquaintance, my dear."

Thackeray's girl flushed charmingly and Elias began to make his way back to the place where the music began.

◆　◆　◆

Josephine opened one eye, for she had smelled the duke approaching before he arrived. He smelled like leather and wealth and sandalwood and . . . she could not believe she was actually waxing poetic in her mind about the scent of a man. She opened the other eye as he sat down again, as if his place was designated next to her on the bench. He of the wild hair and soulful dark hazel eyes, he of the annoying questions.

"Excuse my reach, Your Grace, but I must have access to all the keys."

Her arm brushed his and she cursed the thrill.

"I do not mind, Blue," he said with a quirk of his lips. "And as I said, do call me Elias."

"I am not comfortable with that. The form of address is much too intimate."

"Yes. Intimate. As intimate as you have allowed any man to get here, is it not?"

"Yes."

That was enough of an answer, she thought, to such an intrusive question.

"No one has ever offered you the amount it would take to get you to one of the storied rooms of your Mother Superior?"

"There is no amount. Furthermore—you said you were not trying to bed me."

"I am not. I am merely curious. We have a night to fill with words, and you are uncommonly prickly for someone so concerned with decorum."

"You are baiting me, I think. I can tell from your manner and the lines around your mouth that you were less than decorous in your early years."

"You have been looking at my mouth?" One corner of the offending body part shot up into a smirk. She slipped and missed a chord. "Careful, love. I heard that."

"So you recognize Schubert, Your Grace."

"Elias. I can recognize Schubert from three rooms away. I can even recognize Schubert on a traitorous and vile instrument such as this."

She laughed despite herself. "It is all that I have here."

"A shame. It does a disservice to your talent."

The compliment caught her off guard. She let a few seconds pass by, concentrating on the song.

"Thank you," she said, belated and awkward.

He did not return the politeness but instead sat sipping his brandy and listening to her play. It was a comfort just to have his warmth at her side, his commanding presence. She became aware that a good portion of the room was staring at them. Some of them were whispering. She should have expected that. A duke and the lightskirt pianist: the bluestocking, the one they called uptight and prudish despite her scandalous outfit. Josephine supposed they were right in a way. Sometimes it was an excitement to be in such an uninhibited place, but most of the time she felt deep shame. There was not another way to make a significant amount of money as a female on her own. It was the best and possibly only option. There were bigger dangers at the Dove, though, beyond groping and drunken lewdness. Josephine had a place to go after the club closed, but many other girls were not as lucky. It was a well-known fact that if you slept at the Dove, you were in peril.

"Your playing has become maudlin," the duke's voice rumbled. "What are you thinking?"

"Only that this delightful night has to end," she lied. She supposed she should try to keep the repartee flirtatious, though she was not sure what this solemn man wanted for his money. Couples were starting to wander away and Mother Superior stood at the bar, surveying with a keen eye the progress she was making. Money filled her green eyes; it powered them.

The duke laughed.

"What?" Josephine snapped.

"You are a terrible liar," he smiled, his fingers on the keys. He tinkled a sweeter melody under her so-called maudlin measures. "Did I have to pay extra for honesty?"

She adjusted the tune to match him. More eyes turned their way.

"You came to a brothel expecting honesty?"

"I came here expecting to leave early," he said, "not to correct your choice of compositions. One might think you were playing a requiem right now."

"I am distracted."

"Perhaps you need a drink." He motioned to Mother Superior and she was at their side in a flash. Elias smiled at her in a most cordial way. Josephine noted to herself that she must stop thinking of him by his first name. "My bluestocking is in need of cheering. Might we have a glass of your best wine?"

Mother balked at the suggestion. "The girls know better than to request my private stock."

His eyes narrowed, flashed into hazardous black. Josephine stopped playing, her fingers hovering in time above the keys.

"A duke is requesting."

As the madam slunk away, Josephine dared to look at Elias in the face fully.

"Do you always throw around your title like this?" she whispered.

"Never. Only in extreme situations and your frown, my dear, is an extreme situation."

She could not help but smile at that. Truth be told, she found those hawkish features of his dreadfully handsome. Sitting beside him for so long was putting ideas in her mind that she had not thought herself capable of after long years of observing men of his ilk. His disordered hair was begging her to put her hands in it, to tear the mask from his face, and kiss the tautness from his smirk. *My goodness, where did that thought come from?* She drew in a breath and turned her gaze back to the ivories.

"My friend Lord Thackeray is quite taken with one of your acquaintances. Or, your 'grand friend,' as she called you."

"Yes, Sa—Crimson. They are always together when he is here. I worry that she is getting the wrong impression. I am sure you see the danger in women like us thinking that a nobleman will rescue them from their nightmares. Impractical at best, heartbreaking at worst."

He thought it over for a moment before answering. He was a careful man, she could tell, the kind who weighed his words.

"I know that he likes her very much, and I am sure that she is paid well for the fun they have together. It may be that he is grooming her to be his mistress, but as for far-flung dreams . . . Nicholas's family would never allow a marriage so beneath him."

"I told her as much," Josephine sighed. "But she is young and naive."

The bartender, a grunt of a man who never shaved called Digby, clunked a wine glass in front of Josephine. It sloshed with the force.

"For you, BB," he spat. "And so's you know, the mistress is not happy."

"She should be more than happy with the amount my companion has spent this eve."

"So far," Elias added.

"She don't like demands."

"She likes money," the duke said, palming something to Digby. He smiled a black-toothed approval and walked away.

Josephine took a sip of her wine. It was tart and delicious and the best she'd ever had in the Dove. She savored it before swallowing, thinking over exactly how to say what she needed to next.

"Elias," she began, hoping that the name he wished her to use would soften the blow she had to land. "I know I told you already, but I feel I must reiterate. I am not for sale here. No matter the wine, the compliments, the charm, the unreasonable amount of money you continue to spend . . . I do not allow liberties."

"I heard you the first two times, Blue. I did not come here for a tumble. Though I must admit I have no qualm about paying for the privilege of admiring your legs and your stunning eyes, even behind that ostentatious mask."

This time she gulped the wine. It was easier to take those kinds of comments from men whom she was not attracted to. She had to admit it. She was attracted to the damned cad. He was odd, stoic, nearly uncouth, but she was unaccountably drawn to him. Josephine urged time to go forward as fast as possible, because she could not take much more of the close proximity and wordplay.

"No response? And you seemed so feisty a moment ago."

"Erm . . . thank you."

"What do gentlemen who pay for your company usually talk about?"

"My appearance, much less poetically. Lewd comments and questions about which lady they should choose among the crowd. Consistent pleas to grant a private audience. Complaints about Mother Superior and the alcohol. Demands to know what I look like under my mask. What I look like under my dress."

The room was clearing out, just a smattering of stragglers were left now: women past their prime trying to entice the last of the gentlemen and some hopeless louts who would leave disappointed, with coin still in their pocket. It would be a comfort that there were many other places in seedier parts of the city still open to allay their frustration.

"It sounds terribly depressing."

"It is, Your Grace. You needn't feel sorry for me, however. I would not want your pity." She gestured around the room at the people dispersing. "Mother will be closing up the bar soon, as the couples have gone off two by two or three. I hope you do not feel cheated out of your money."

"Not in the least." He picked up her hand as if to kiss it, but then just ran a thumb over her palm, looking at her too keenly. The tactile buzz of it was shocking. She imagined she could feel every line of his finger graze her skin.

"It was . . . a lovely evening."

"Indeed it was."

Josephine stopped herself just short of asking if she would be seeing him again. What a stupid, impractical, girlish question to pop into her mind. She held his gaze too long, mesmerized, and then pulled her hand back to finish her wine in one swig. She was not looking forward to settling accounts with Mother this evening.

"Have you a way home?" Elias asked.

"I will rent a hackney, as I do every night. That is, after I give Mother Superior her well-earned cut of your ill-spent money."

"Allow me to drive you home in my carriage."

She actually guffawed. "I am sorry—Your Grace—but a woman from a brothel getting a ride home from a duke would cause quite a stir. It is uncommonly good of you, but I cannot."

He looked hurt.

"You do not want me to know where you live."

He was damned astute. She thought her excuse still stood as well; there was no societal way it would ever be accepted. Someone would see and someone would talk. There was a moment where they were just staring at each other. She could see those absurdly deep brown eyes considering how long the argument would be to convince her otherwise. She could see the moment that he knew she would not give in. There was an odd look of respect on his face after that.

"Do not let the wench take too much of your money, Blue."

"I have no control over that," she told him with a sad smile. "Farewell, Elias."

One last impropriety.

"For now, yes." He stood and bowed, holding his hat instead of putting it on his head. It was almost as if he was stalling.

Josephine scraped to her feet and curtsied rather without a stitch of grace. She took a good look at the wolfish and sensual face that she was sure she would never see again. She had a wild premonition that he was going to sweep her into his arms—whatsoever was wrong with her racing thoughts? Josephine shifted, trying to break his heavy gaze without being obvious. She could daydream about him, perhaps cast him in the novels she read at voracious speed. Unlike Sally, she would not hold out hope that this particular nobleman was anything but a strange hiccup in her normal routine.

"Good evening," she forced out.

The next day, she was sure it would be like it had never happened.

CHAPTER TWO

"Foxhunting, as a so-called sport, does not have much to recommend it. If it serves only as a social activity, I can think of many examples that would involve more merriment and less blood. I do not think it bold of me to wonder if the hounds and the gentlemen are not too far apart in personality and I ask you, do we not have ambition to be more than merely dogs?"
—FROM *THE COLLECTED ESSAYS OF LORD ELIAS ADDISON*

Elias was groggy in the morning, staring into his dressing mirror. He was trying to remember the dream he had been pulled out of, one of a piano and miles of fabric dropping to the floor. His valet fussed around him, muttering muted curses about the state of his hair.

"Are you certain you will not take more time with your hair today? Perhaps I can trim it? Her Grace expects you to accompany her to the market and you know how she hates you frowzy."

"Yes, of course, I 'look like a wild man.' My mother will have to accept me as I am if she wants to go to Cheapside this morning. She could just take Alessandra like usual."

"I believe the duchess wants to speak with you, Your Grace."

Of course, why take his sister when the duchess could use the time to criticize her son alone?

"She wants to speak at me, not with me."

Elias regarded his countenance. He was glad to be out of mourning clothes. The black had become stifling. The navy chosen by Dryden suited him much better. His cravat sat starched brilliantly white on his dressing table.

"You may go, Dryden," he dismissed his valet, who frowned with disapproval.

"But your cravat, my lord . . ."

"Yes, yes," Elias waved a hand. "You have made it clear that you find it improper, and you would rather take care of it. However, you may go."

He sank down into a chair and let out a long sigh, one that he would only release when alone. Elias hated Cheapside, he hated shopping, and he especially hated wasting the day away. He wanted to finish searching his father's study. James Addison had a habit of hiding papers that he thought might be embarrassing: bills of sale for things bought for his courtesans over the years, deeds for city houses bought for the same. Elias was exaggerating when he complained that his father had frittered away the fortune—and he would only complain to Thackeray. The duchy of Lennox had so much money that his father's debauches could not put a dent in it, but Elias was annoyed nonetheless. The farms around the Lennox country estate were not suffering greatly, but his father had done little to improve their situation. As the new duke, Elias intended to fix this, to give his young sister Alessandra the London debut she deserved, and take up his seat in the House of Lords. He had plans that did not include finding a wife immediately.

It was inevitable that was what his mother wanted to talk about on this little trip.

He picked up his cravat and began to tie it into a mathematical knot, hoping that the tight angle would hold his head on his neck as he listened to Sophia natter on endlessly about finding the proper woman and making an heir. She had already been on Elias to pair off before James died, but now that he was gone and there was no successor, she had ratcheted up her efforts. She believed he was far too old to be unmarried, as did the patronesses who threw every available lady in his path each time he attended a ball.

He would eventually marry. He had no choice. It was just that he refused to believe that any of the women—to be more accurate, girls— would be happy living with a man of his demeanor. He could already see himself beginning to resent their tittering. The woman he would marry would be the one he would sit across the breakfast and dinner table from for the rest of his life, and he did not want a life where he was silent and bitter. He had seen that dynamic during his childhood, James and Sophia ingesting their meals and then parting ways. It had much to do with James's behavior, but Elias knew that Sophia's conduct had also played a part.

There were many times he wished to have been born a stable boy, where his choices could be his own. His sister said he would have made a terrible farm lad; with his face, the wolves would think he was one of their own. That Alessandra was going to be quite a catch for some man, some day.

Elias's mother never knocked. She would never think her admittance was not welcome, even in his private chambers.

"Do hurry, darling boy. I want there to be fresh flowers when we arrive at the market, and we still have not had breakfast. Alessandra is not feeling well, so she cannot accompany us today."

"How convenient," he muttered, examining his mother's still stylish mourning gown and her elaborate hairstyle. She was powdered and painted to an outlandish level. She would never be seen in public looking anything less than the most expensive widowed duchess. Truly, she had always looked much younger than she was in reality. It had only gotten worse since his father's death . . . she was still a beautiful woman for her age, and he suspected that she was starting to look for a male companion. He shuddered inwardly. It was none of his business.

"I expect you downstairs in ten minutes," she chirped. "Dryden will have the phaeton ready for our trip as soon as we finish dining."

"Yes, Mother."

After a hurried breakfast where he listened to his mother chatter about what she intended to purchase and how she hoped it would not rain, Elias sat unhappily in the phaeton, wondering how he would make it through this journey.

◆   ◆   ◆

"Four crates arrived today, Josie!" Sally exclaimed. Though she was known as Crimson at the Dove, she was just Sally Hopewell at the Paper Garden. "Four crates of new books and some old ones that look like they'll be worth some money!"

Perhaps she could be excited about the prospect of new inventory, but Josephine only saw more things to put away and sort through. Her back was aching, not only from sitting rigid at the piano last night to not shame the duke with her poor posture, but from shifting tomes back and forth while trying to arrange the front window to entice shoppers. There were not many who stopped in before passing by.

Josephine looked around her bookstore and let out a long breath of air. Mother Superior had taken over half the money that Elias had given to her last night. She did not mind as much, because it had been an interesting evening, but the money was becoming even more necessary. As it stood, the combination of money from the Dove and the Garden was barely keeping her afloat. Having Sally around helped, and the poor girl really had no other option. Orphans like herself were especially vulnerable at the Sleeping Dove. On the nights that certain groups of men came in and girls disappeared forever, it was always a girl without family who fell victim to them.

"You're worrying again," Sally remarked, fussing with a stack of books to be delivered to infirm customers. "Don't be anxious. I'm just sure things will turn around."

"You are being far too optimistic. Too like your Lord Thackeray. He is filling your head with nonsense."

The bells jingled to announce a customer, an overly made-up and obviously wealthy woman who looked as if she was trying to compensate for her advanced age with a mass of face powder. She was doing a sufficient job of it, Josephine thought to herself, but some of the age lines could not be hidden. Trailing behind her was a tall man in a crisp velvet-lined overcoat, smelling of . . . sandalwood and leather and wealth. Josephine cursed and turned away. Of all the bloody rotten luck. It simply could not be him. What would he be doing here?

"I am finally ready to read some of this Miss Austen material," the woman declared. "I cannot be so ill-informed when other ladies start talking for one moment longer."

"Of course we can help you with that, Lady . . . ?" Sally began.

"The Duchess of Lennox."

"Oh! I am so sorry, Your Grace!" Sally fell into a sloppy curtsey. "Please accept my sincere apologies."

Lennox, Josephine noted. *The Duke of Lennox*. And a wife. A decorated, aged wife who was at least fifteen years older than him. She must have been frothing with money, rich enough for the duke to overlook her age. Or they were in love, which sent a buzz of horror straight through Josephine. She tried to shake her head to clear it, but found that nothing on her would move. She was frozen in her spot, though it would have taken her less than thirty seconds to show the duchess where any number of editions of Austen were and only moments more to tell her the pros and cons of each. However, there was no way she was turning around for fear of catching his eye. There was no way she could see his dignified, classical face without a mask. It was not an image she wanted in her memory. She certainly did not want to see him standing stalwartly next to his wife. Sally's eyes slid toward her as recognition dawned on her as well.

Josephine found that her legs awakened at the thought of having to face him in the daylight. She tried to slink away.

"I hear this shop has a fine rare books room," Elias's deep voice intoned. Josephine heard it in her sternum, reverberating through her and bouncing off all of the walls of her insides. It felt like arrows shot from fifty paces, true to their target. She clutched her petticoat with white knuckles. "Perhaps while the duchess browses, your other shop girl would kindly direct me to it."

"Ah, Your Grace! Miss Grant is the proprietress of this fine establishment, no mere employee. I am sure she would be proud to show off the collection of rare books we have amassed."

Proud was not exactly the word, Josephine thought. Aghast was much more appropriate. She saw that she had no choice now but to turn around and smile as if there was nothing at all wrong. She should be pleased to have a member of the nobility in her store. Her fake smile overpowered her face as she wracked her brain to find a reason to stay silent. There was a chance he would recognize her voice, even though it was less husky than the tone she used at the Sleeping Dove.

"If you please, Yer Grace—follow me, right this way," she said, significantly higher and much more Cockney than her ladylike upbringing. Sally gave her a queer look at the sound of it. She saw no recognition in Elias's eyes, just a strange detachment from his surroundings. It was a relief and a disappointment to find she was beneath his notice. He had a ducal comportment; she had seen it many times before. Out in the light of the day, he looked colder and more closed off. His posture was stick straight and all very proper. No one would have ever guessed he had spent the last evening at a brothel. Unfortunately, she still found him handsome. It was dashed inconvenient.

He followed along the hallway, stylish Hessian boots clicking on the stones. She had to remind herself to breathe. She reasoned that there was little chance he would recognize her eyes or lips or voice—he had been drinking at the time, and he was a duke. He surely met scads of women on a daily basis and they would blend together. Her backup plan, she decided, would be to play the innocent. This was, of course, a delicate way of saying that she would deny everything.

"'Ere you are, Yer Grace," she said in the ridiculous accent. "I'll leave you to examine at cher leisure."

Elias picked up a book, glanced at it, examined her with a piercing stare, and set it back down again. A tempting smile debuted on his mouth. It was altogether more daring than any she had seen the night before.

"Blue."

She coughed, a rather harsh expelling of air.

"I'm afraid the books are not organized by color, but by author or series."

"No, Bluestocking. You. Blue. I did not expect to see you so soon. You are irresistible without your mask, even in that atrocious day gown."

"I do apologize—I think you must have mistaken me for someone else. Being rather plain—"

"You are far from plain."

"—it happens all the time. Now, you will understand if I return to my shop. It is not proper for us to be alone in this place together."

"It is not, indeed."

He had advanced inches while she stammered and now stood in front of her. They were face to face, unmasked, unlike the night before. The cheekbones that had disappeared under the black fabric now directed her attention to the eyes that so vexed her. The passion in them was unnerving, exciting, too much for her to face in stark daylight.

"I like your face much better without the mask. It was in the way," he murmured. "So, you own a bookstore. Quite surprising, I did not expect that you would be a businesswoman. Are you really a part of that horrid Bluestocking society? Do you stomp about demanding rights and such? I like the image of you as a crusader. Really, love, I just like the image of you in general."

"I am sure I do not know what you are talking about." Josephine nearly fell backward over a stack of books trying to lean away from him. He caught her hand and pulled her in, his other hand snaking around her back to support her. She was stable again, but he did not let go. He kissed her wrist instead of her fingers, lingering. Somehow, his lips on her wrist were a thousand times more intimate than any kiss on the hand.

"I . . . do not. You. Cannot. You are . . ."

A rake. Trying to seduce her while his wife browsed for books.

"I am Elias Addison, the Duke of Lennox. And you are?"

She stumbled over a box behind her, wriggling to release herself from the embrace.

"I thank you for your patronage, it is truly an honor," she sputtered, the words coming out in a rush, each fighting for supremacy over the ones that came before. "I trust that you will bring anything you wish to purchase to the front counter. Thank you." When she finished, she staggered to the door and closed it behind her, far harder than she intended.

She closed the door in the face of a duke.

◆　◆　◆

Elias had never had a door slammed on him. Never, ever in his life. Wherever he went, doors opened. Looking at the worn wood that Blue had shut against his onslaught, he began to laugh. He laughed long and hard, doubling over, the longest he had laughed since the death of his father. All the irritation he had felt at his mother for insisting on stopping at the tacky little store called the Paper Garden, a ladies' bookstore, for heaven's sake, drained from him. He could simply hug her

29

for it now, that wonderful idea of patronizing this dilapidated book-seller in Cheapside, when there were perfectly good gentlemen's shops he would rather give his money to. Or so he had said. Whatever stroke of luck brought him here, he blessed it. He had been looking at the eyes of every lady they passed that day, but until the shopkeep turned around, he had failed to find the unique blue-grey. He found it amusing that she would even try to pretend she was someone else. There was no way he could forget the unique antisymmetry of her face, the way that the near-constant furrow in her brow threw off her features, slanted her. It was quite fetching. He wanted to see her when she was not on her guard, to know what she looked like when she was content. He was not fool enough to assume this was on the horizon any time soon.

So the Bawdy Bluestocking was the proprietress of her own shop, selling lurid novels to ladies in the front and more esoteric fare in the back, from the looks of the shelves around him. He spied Pope and Crabbe, Shakespeare, of course, and names he did not recognize at all. He wondered how she chose her stock and where it came from. She must spend her days in endless research. The thought was unaccountably lovely to him. Not exactly reading for delicate sensibilities, all of this—he saw books on Hermeticism to his right—but he was learning that he couldn't take anything about this woman at face value. It was refreshing for such a mystery to be presented to him. He wanted to unravel her in numerous ways.

Earlier, while his mother looked at dress patterns and lace, Elias had mulled over whether or not to return to the Sleeping Dove in the evening. Thackeray had sent word that there would be a special show they would not want to miss, so he knew where he would be, come nine o'clock. It was a fine respite from days mired in the property, but as a practical man, Elias knew that what was happening between he and Blue was a dodgy thing. He could not seem to stop himself from baiting her, to see the color rise in her cheeks. Their fingers together on the piano against the black and white keys led his thoughts to moving those digits elsewhere and the interesting positions one could achieve on the bench in his personal chambers . . .

He gave his head a violent shake. When he was young, he was often chastised for letting his imagination run away from him and now that he was older, he could see the curse of it. Images of the bluestocking consumed his brain, too vivid, from the compromising to the mundane—reading together by candlelight, snuffing those same candles to retire to bed for more physical pleasures.

"Lennox!"

His mother's voice from behind the door snapped him back to reality.

"I have finished my shopping, so do stop browsing," she called. "I have a milliner's appointment at the top of the hour."

"Damnation," he muttered, looking down at himself with slight discomfiture. He grabbed an ugly yellow book large enough to shield his fervor for the few moments it would take to get himself under control. He felt like a silly adolescent boy.

The duchess was waiting impatiently outside.

"You were not in such a rush just moments ago, Mother."

"This place is so very dusty," she sneered, her skirts swooshing as she made her way back to the large front room.

Blue was nowhere to be found. Likely she had fled to an inner sanctum or left the premises. He was grateful for that, being that his ardor had just cooled and he doubted he could keep it that way if he saw her again. They paid for their books by way of the friendly sales girl, who was also the legendary Crimson. He gave her a secret smile, but she was chirpy and nervous. Elias let his mother exit before turning briefly backward.

"If you would, miss, may I have the name of your employer? I would like to send along a note of thanks for all of her help."

The girl giggled.

"I thought you knew, Your Grace. You bought her book."

Elias looked down at the title in his hand: *On Society's Ills and the Real Price of Prostitution*, by Josephine Grant.

◆   ◆   ◆

"He did what?" Josephine demanded.

"He bought your book, lovey. But I don't think he even knew you were the author until I told him." Sally appeared nonplussed by Josephine's rage. "I really don't understand the problem. You wanted more people to read it, you put it with the more serious books. So, if a duke reads it and agrees, perhaps he will tell others."

Josephine sank into a reading chair, finding no comfort in the cushions that were designed precisely for that purpose.

"Oh, Sal. That man is exactly the irredeemable rake I wrote the book about. Bored, stuck in an arranged marriage, a patron of houses of ill repute. You saw him at the Dove last night."

"Flirting outrageously with the piano player!" Sally clutched her hands together at her chest, theatrical as always. She had aspirations of Drury Lane, that one. "Oh, dear! I've told a handsome and fabulously rich duke who is interested in your charms who you are. Heaven save us!"

"He recognized me." Josephine slammed a fist on the arm of the chair. "Bloody hell, he knows who I am. He knows my blasted name."

"I always said you'd better use a nom de plume."

"You know my opinion of that. There are too many books by 'A Lady' circulating now. I have no idea how to even catalogue them anymore." She tugged on a piece of her hair, nervous.

"Perhaps you shouldn't go to the Dove tonight," Sally said with a tinge of worry.

Josephine sighed the fat sigh, the one she reserved for dire situations, the one that expanded to fill entire rooms. This room, for certain, and perhaps the whole block.

"That is impossible. I have to play tonight for Mother Superior's annual pageant; she would murder me if I missed it. It is a highly anticipated event. You know we both have to go." She stared at the wall, the weight of her actions finally settling in her gut. "What a fool I am."

"No, no, Josie! Never say that! You are the bravest woman I have ever known. You do *real* good. Most so-called accomplished ladies simply play at charity work."

Josephine never felt like it was charity work. It felt strange that Sally should call it that. Women's lives were on the line and Josephine had found a way she could help. Over time, it had become obvious that the mysterious disappearance of girls from the brothel was connected with the appearance of certain groups of men that Mother Superior fawned over. If you watched the crowd, which Josephine did, you could figure out what girl they set their sights on. Always an orphan, always homeless, always without family or friends. It was nearly guaranteed that if a susceptible girl spent the night at the Dove when those men visited, she would be gone on the morrow and Mother's pockets would be flush.

From what Josephine could glean, Mother Superior had at least three groups of gentlemen with whom these transactions occurred, gentlemen with noble titles and exotic proclivities. She didn't know what they were doing with the girls, but since none were ever heard from again, she had to assume that they had not met a good end. So, Josephine did what she thought anyone with the means would: she started taking in girls who had nowhere else to go. The Paper Garden was cramped, stifling, and smelled of rotting books, but it was a place to stay.

She had begun writing *On Society's Ills* as she slowly learned of Mother Superior's hidden purposes. It was written from a place of anger at the world she lived in and published in a foolish fit of optimism. Josephine had never thought that a patron of the Dove would read the book, but now it was in the duke's hands. He knew where they lived and worked.

"This has to stop," Josephine declared. "We cannot allow Lennox to sniff around here. Who knows if he is connected to one of the gentlemen Mother works with?"

"That seems unlikely," Sally said, brow furrowed. "He's Nicholas's friend and we know that Nic is not one of them. Besides, if he wants to pursue you, how would you presume to stop him?"

Josephine picked up her cup of tea and started up the staircase. "I'll think of something."

CHAPTER THREE

"The men of the nobility often become bored with their lives of leisure and excess of money, so they must find an outlet to manufacture drama in their lives. Instead of working to improve our great country, they waste away, drunk on both liquor and power in houses of ill repute. But what of the women that serve them in these establishments? Much is said of the plight of the noble lady, but what of her sister in the gutters within earshot of the bells of St. Mary's?"

—FROM *ON SOCIETY'S ILLS AND THE REAL PRICE OF PROSTITUTION* BY JOSEPHINE GRANT

Elias left his mother at the clothier's and went back to Ashworth Hall. He spent the majority of the afternoon reading the high-and-mighty ideas of one Miss Grant, a bluestocking indeed. He doubted she was actually a member of the society, but she had some radical social ideas. He was surprised that this tome had not caused a scandal upon release. He realized why when he looked at the imprint—Paper Garden Press. Bold little Blue was publishing by herself.

Thackeray called on him promptly at eight o'clock, in an unmarked carriage they had used for raking hell back before Elias became the duke.

"The girls will dance tonight," Nicholas told him with anticipation, "and certainly not the dances we are used to in stifling ballrooms."

"Even the bluestocking?"

"Alas, no. Someone has to play the music."

Elias pushed down the disappointment he felt.

Upon arriving at the Dove, they drank until donning the omnipresent masks. He was as anxious as he had been on the first night, but now with anticipation instead of dread. He could not wait to confront Josephine, if simply to see the look on her face when she realized that he had read her precious manifesto. Elias allowed himself to get a little drunker than he should, but it had not calmed his nerves one whit. Mother Superior's cloying greeting was lost on him as he scanned the crowd for a pair of blue stockings.

She was nowhere to be found.

Sally, however, was already on her way to the open arms of Nicholas. She was dressed more elaborately than the night before, gleaming with jewels that were so plentiful that they had to be fake. That did not seem to matter to Nicholas, who embraced her in full view of the crowd. Either he had too much confidence in the masks, or he simply did not care.

"Your Grace!" Sally greeted Elias, her breath half stolen by the grinning Nicholas. "It's a pleasure to see you again so soon. It's a special night, our annual Birds of Eden Pageant!"

"How will you have a show without a piano player?" he asked, thinking it a clever way to inquire without conveying his worry.

Her face fell.

"We are a little worried. BB hasn't shown up yet nor has she sent word, and we've under an hour until show time. She's never late. I do hope nothing's happened."

Elias knew that something had happened—the something that passed between them when he kissed the soft skin of her wrist. She would not be coming back to the Sleeping Dove. Not tonight and perhaps never again. Foolishly, he had scared her.

The moment he had come to that conclusion, the woman in question stepped out from behind a curtain that shielded the place where the ladies donned their supposed finery. She looked far from scared; she seethed with unholy rage. It lit her eyes from behind with a new fire as she scanned the crowd, just as he had done previously. When those points of furious blue found him, they narrowed. He had been targeted.

"Thank heaven!" Sally exclaimed. "There she is!"

Josephine towered, glittered, head to toe in flowing silk except the slice in the gown to expose her blue stockings. She was still looking straight at him, making sure that he saw her gaze and expression. Then she turned abruptly and went to the piano.

"Lennox," Nicholas said carefully. "Did the Bawdy Bluestocking just cut you?"

"Direct." His voice came out calmer than he expected. "She gave me the cut direct."

Sally was silent and visibly anxious.

Elias could understand that he had taken liberties where he should not have, but there was no excuse for what she had done. There was no excuse in the world to give the cut direct to a duke. He could not remember a time that anyone had dared to do it to him, but he had seen it many times in ballrooms. It was the worst possible snub, this looking directly at a person and then away. It said wordlessly, *I see you, but you are below my notice.* Elias knew he should not dignify it, but his feet were moving before his mind could rationalize.

◆　◆　◆

Josephine sat down at her bench and let out the breath she had been holding in since laying eyes on the haughty Duke of Lennox in the crowd. She had not been sure he would show up, especially if he had started reading her book. He would know why she spent a great deal of her nights at the Dove, and he could probably infer what she was doing. Many parts of the book alluded to the nefarious aspects of the Dove, though it did not name them nor did it name the establishment. He was a sharp man, for someone raised in nobility. He was not as soft-skulled as the peers of her previous acquaintance, but he was miles more self-important.

Proven by the fact that he was currently stalking over to her.

"Of all the—" he started.

With all the composure she could muster, she faced him, one finger in the air to stop his assault of words.

"Your Grace. I am not being paid to speak with you this evening. I must practice the introduction, as the girls are counting on me to help them present their wares to their best advantage."

"Hypocrite," he snarled.

"Hardly," she returned. She plumped her skirts to settle down and touch the keys. "You are one to talk, in that case. Now, if you will allow me . . ."

He would not. He was puffed up, fixing to make a scene.

"How. Dare. You," he roared, using the booming ducal voice that Josephine thought must be a class in itself at Eton. He slammed a twenty pound note on the piano. "That should be enough for a serious conversation, Bluestocking, no more of this idiocy. Now move over."

Josephine thought for a moment about kicking him in his most sensitive spot and then thought the better of it. Besides, the ever-watchful Mother Superior saw the money and the man. Josephine moved over a mere sliver so that the damned Duke of damned Lennox would be uncomfortable when he sat down.

"Very accommodating of you, Miss Grant," he scoffed. He played some test chords on the high keys and his face showed his extreme displeasure. "This instrument is just so appalling."

"You address me by my surname, and oh! Thank you, Your Grace, for your discretion! It is safe to assume that you know the book you bought was authored by me."

"Oh, yes," he said, raising a sinister eyebrow. "I most undoubtedly do."

He kept playing, wincing at the wrongness of the sound. Even warming up, she could tell he had true talent. She had never known a man of nobility who wished to put in the practice that playing well took, but this man was an oddity in so many ways. Every time he leaned for a farther key, he gained more ground, making sure that he had his share of the bench. Josephine moved another inch to her left so that they were not touching.

"Then you must understand that I cannot continue hosting you in this way." She lowered her voice. "And you may never come to my store again."

"They," he glanced up, looking around the room, causing dozens of eyes to skitter away. "They think me a lovesick fool, coming over here after you cut me, in full view of a quarter of the beau monde. Grant me an explanation, Miss Grant."

"Explanations are too expensive, Lennox. Even for a duke." She hoped he would take the use of his title as she intended, as a slight, hear the contempt in her voice. He did: the slender raise of his left eyebrow told her so. "Now, if you will excuse me, the show will be starting soon. I will thank you to take your seat with Lord Thackeray."

He crossed his arms, like a great thundercloud over her.

"I will not have the assembled crowd think that I play your fool, Josephine, and I do not think your mother would like you pushing me off my perch." He nodded over to Mother Superior, watching with great curiosity, but at a distance, near the bar. "For both of our sakes, do try to make this look like a lovers' quarrel."

"She is not my mother. You impede my reach on the piano," she muttered stubbornly. "Besides, I doubt you brought enough flush to pay for something like that."

Elias finally uncrossed his arms with a sideways tilt of his head.

"All you think about is money."

Her fingers froze on the keys as she tried to contain the rage she felt at the serious expression in his blasted beautiful eyes. She thought it might be sympathy, which repulsed her.

"I am sorry if you find me crass, but I do not have the leisure time as afforded Your Grace. Or any man." She shuffled through the sheet music in front of her, searching for the intro measures, and found that her eyes were watering. Embarrassed, surely. Burned. The libretto was a convenient excuse to turn her face. "I do not want your censure or your pity."

"I didn't mean—"

"Shhh," she cooed, in a tone she usually reserved to pacify drunkards. "The ladies are waiting for me to play the introduction."

Josephine began the overture and Elias flagged down Digby, to order drinks for the both of them. He made no attempt to move from the bench, but he did lean back a bit to accommodate her playing. She shifted, adjusted her posture, tried to focus. It was dastardly hard to do, knowing that he could see the composition, and in the absolute holiness of his arrogance he would not hesitate to correct a mistake. He was watching her, from what she could make out in her peripheral vision, but she could not see his exact expression. Foul man, who should be home with his wife, instead here he was, making her life ever more difficult. This was the exact reason she railed against the nobility in her book. The men had nothing to do but indulge their basest desires, whether or not they ruined lives in the process.

He flipped the page for her as she reached the end of the intro.

"Can you play and talk at the same time?" he asked, too near her ear.

"In general," she said, staring straight forward at the bars and notes, not daring to turn. "But this arrangement is a bit new to me, so I need to concentrate." She obeyed the long rest at the end of the measure, hearing the girls shuffle behind the curtain. Josephine knew to wait until they calmed down to play the opening song. The duke stood up, apparently deciding to honor her request for attentiveness.

"Apologize for cutting me," he murmured, bending so that only she could hear his words in the silent anticipation of the room waiting for dancing girls. Or was it silent because everyone was staring at them? She played an innocuous line to try to cover and distract, but Elias's lips were still next to her ear. "Apologize, and see me after the show. Alone."

"No," she said through set teeth.

To her absolute horror, he placed a hand on her chin and turned her face to him. With her sitting and being forced to look up, he seemed impossibly tall and breathtakingly handsome.

"You will," he all but whispered. "Won't you?"

"Go. Away. Now."

His face broke into a smile, a genuine one.

"Are you implying that if I go away *now*, you will see me *later*?"

The man was not going to back down. She would have to lie to him and find a way to escape after the show.

"Fine, Lennox. Fine. Go!"

Mother Superior was waving from behind the makeshift stage. Josephine had to start. Everyone in the place was gaping at them. They had become the preshow.

"Go!" She hissed once more.

She could have sworn he was chuckling when he walked away.

◆　◆　◆

"Are you mad?" Nicholas demanded when Elias returned to the table in front. There was a stifled laugh within the question.

"Quite," Elias said. He felt light-headed and exhilarated. For a man who lived by rules that were set down ages before he had any say about the matter, and lived them to the letter, to fence with this woman was novel and invigorating. He was not doing it for anyone but himself, a feeling that he had not experienced since being snatched from Oxford three years before. If there was talk, he would have to worry about it later. He wanted the brief moment of happiness that he felt when he saw the spark in her eyes.

She did not hate him. She just wanted to.

"Lennox, you rakehell. You practically kissed her in front of everyone."

"An exaggeration."

Nicholas sighed with happiness. "It does my heart good to see you enjoying yourself."

"You have always had an exceptional gift for hyperbole," Elias frowned, noting that ears around their table had perked up. "I needed to put the girl in her place."

"Which place is that?" Nicholas chortled. "Your bed?"

"She is impertinent, Thackeray," he said with as much gravity as he could muster, though he was still smiling. "Behave, watch the show. Here comes your Crimson, in fact."

As Nicholas's paramour took the stage, Digby set down a much-needed brandy in front of Elias. He drank deeply and then craned his neck to make sure that Blue had gotten her wine. He had paid a handsome fee for Digby's services and for Mother to leave them alone, and he intended to get his money's worth. The expensive wine sat on the pianoforte, untouched. Josephine had her head down as she played. He meant to look away, but her loose hair fell over her neck in such a way that he found his gaze locked. He mentally traced the line of her collarbone, so high and defined.

She glanced up and he smiled, bashfully, which was an odd emotion for him. Something about it pleased her and she returned the smile.

He was ruined.

"Bloody schoolboy," Nicholas whispered, chuckling.

Elias kicked him under the table and he let out a little *oof*.

"Mind the stage show, Nicholas, for Sally will ask your opinion."

Elias himself could not attend the stage show at all. He closed his eyes and let Josephine's notes wash over him unaccompanied by images. He drained the remainder of his cognac. It was refilled soon enough after, then twenty minutes after that. How long could this show be? It was utterly boring to him, as girl after girl paraded in front of them. Interminable group numbers. Bawdy skits. At least the musical accompaniment was exquisite, though it was hard to hear over the unruly men.

He found that he was getting pleasantly drunk, which in turn made him feel more charitable about the cut direct he had received from that gorgeous creature. It was a misunderstanding. They would talk after she played, and he would be able to tell her that the ideas in her book had a certain clarity that he did not exactly disagree with and that he was not one of the "oblivious" nobility, as she had termed it. It was a damned good thing that no one seemed to patronize her bookstore. If another duke had read the book, the whole of her supply would be set on fire in the public square.

His eyes snapped open. What a feverish idiot he had been to not think of this before—Josephine had used her real name on her book. How was it that she used a careful pseudonym at the club but was so careless with her real reputation? She had been lucky up to that point, but it could not continue. The wrong person would happen upon the book; it was inevitable. Her bookstore would be in jeopardy for certain, her person as well, perhaps. The book was not just radical in its social implications; it was a condemnation of the entire upper echelon. What Josephine was doing was both dangerous and imprudent.

The music was reaching a crescendo, the finale being all of the girls dancing together in a haphazard manner. It did not look as if they had rehearsed long. Some tottered; some peeked at their companions to find their place in the steps. Elias set his glass down with heavy-lidded eyes. The good mood he had been cultivating was rent to shreds on the thought of Josephine being in peril. There would be no flirting after the show. There would be a serious conversation, whether she liked it or not.

The show ended with the girls dancing off of the stage and into the crowd, picking their favorite men or being plucked away by a greedy eye. It was no time at all before Sally and Thackeray found each other. Just as Elias was about to get up, a painted face and bejeweled dress landed in his lap.

"Where are you off to, Duke?" purred the woman, her eyes lined thick with kohl. "The bluestocking told me earlier that you would be in need of company this evening. Perhaps I could provide you with some comfort?"

Elias twisted to see the piano. Blast. She was gone, with the wine too, that minx. How could she have disappeared without his knowledge? He had not been able to keep his eyes off of her for much of the night.

The girl in his lap was savvy. She followed his gaze to the piano and then took his chin in her hand to turn his eyes back.

"The piano player deserves a break after such a fine performance, wouldn't you say, Your Grace?" She put her arms around his neck, slinky and seductive. "But I can accommodate your desires, darling."

Elias shifted under her with discomfort. She was indeed pretty, but every word out of her mouth made him think of *On Society's Ills and the Real Price of Prostitution*. Josephine had written with startling lucidity on the ways that women fooled themselves when they were forced to sell their bodies to men and their limited income alternatives. The calculated breath on his ear, the way this woman's leg wrapped around the chair, even the smell of her hair . . . it no longer seemed to be the simple charm of a lady. It was calculated for survival. He cleared his throat.

"I have unfinished business with the musician."

"Your money would be spent more wisely elsewhere, you know," she pouted.

He patted her hand chastely. "You are amiable, my dear, but you cannot possibly have what I want."

"Are you certain?" Two bats of her eyelashes.

"Yes. Unless . . ." Elias felt a light go on in his brain, such that it almost seemed visible. "Unless you know where she would go if she wanted to hide."

She looked away, unsure.

"I will pay for your trouble."

Her close-mouthed smile was an answer. Elias stopped to speak with Sally, as he had an important question for her. Then, it was off to find his reckless bluestocking.

◆   ◆   ◆

Behind the ratty rooms in which Mother Superior's girls earned their bread was a small courtyard, lit only by the slivers of moonlight leaking in from an adjacent alleyway. Mother had allowed it to fall into disrepair, but Josephine never minded the fact that it ran wild. Ambitious vines escaped over the walls, so unlike most of the girls inside. Unidentified greenery dotted the stones with no one to weed it out. The only noises were occasional exaggerated moaning from the rooms and vagrants rummaging behind the building.

No one came back here except her, and she was glad of it.

Josephine lit a small cigar from a flickering candlestick, which promptly guttered out. She exhaled and let herself slump against the wall, not caring about the dew on the foliage. The glass of wine, which was her reward for tolerating the duke, stung the back of her throat perfectly. For a moment, she could forget.

"Bollocks," she sighed to herself.

"Smoking, swearing," said a voice from the entryway. "One would not think there was a lady back here."

An unmistakable voice.

Josephine leaned her head back against the wall in frustration.

"Go back to Ashworth Hall, Lennox. There is much in need of your attention and none of it involves being in a brothel."

"You have done your research. Do you know more about me than I know about you, love?"

He hovered, not coming nearer. It was unnerving and evasive, but from what she did know of him, he was a decisive and immovable man. Sally had asked around that afternoon, quizzing the thin flock of customers about the Duke of Lennox.

"As much as I could."

This was not much, but he did not need to know that. There had been no time and the most the people of Cheapside knew about Lennox was that no one really knew him. All that Sally had been able to glean was the previous duke had recently passed and his heir, Elias Addison, prowled the estate, rifling through his predecessor's papers and barely sleeping. One of the ladies, a street flower girl, was ardent about the one time she had seen him in a carriage—"He is like a gothic hero, haunted and all!" His hooded eyes alone could have told her that. Society finds him intimidating and taciturn, said the lovely modiste from the end of the block. The gossip had not yielded much more than Josephine could have guessed within the first two minutes of meeting Lennox.

"I like your book," he said from the dark.

"Like?"

"Like, yes. Of course, it has its problems."

"Oh?"

"Your editor is hasty. Your publisher is untested."

"Good show. You have it all figured out." She put the cigar between her fingers and flicked it, as cheeky as she could muster under his scrutiny. "Take it to the floor of Parliament, won't you?"

"I would never. You hold yourself like a sailor, and I admit that I am frightened of your wrath."

There was a smile coloring his voice as he moved to lean beside her. He shed his mask and she thought he must have been aware that he placed himself in the most flattering spot of moonlight. It had to be calculated, this arrangement of his myriad attributes. The splash of light caught the angles of his cheekbones, the arch of his brows, threw shadows over them, loved them. The lighter streaks of his brown hair glowed, glinted, and reflected off of the stones. She felt sick but not lovesick. Revolted. As Salieri must have felt toward Mozart—this man had been given gifts that he did not deserve and could never live up to.

"Biographical information on the author of the book is sparse," he continued, as if he had not just surrounded himself with a halo of unearthliness. "The leaf says that Josephine Grant lives in Cheapside and lists the address of your store. Why in God's name would you not use an alias, Miss Grant?"

Elias made no move toward her. There was no seduction in his gaze. The answer to his question, that she *was* using an alias, was so simple that she could only guffaw, which she covered by swallowing the rest of her wine for fortification.

Even Sally, her dearest friend, didn't know that she lived her life under a false identity. She had given up any claim to peerage when her father died and she assumed the name Josephine Grant so that she could run the Paper Garden. She even had letters mailed from Scotland to her cousins, telling of her quiet life. Her remaining relatives still lived in Staffordshire and probably did not think about her much, except lingering embarrassment over the reprehensible behavior of her father.

"You could have at least published under BB," he continued. "It might have been a wonderful means of advertisement. If you let word slip out that the exotic and mysterious Bawdy Bluestocking of the Sleeping Dove had written a protest paper against prostitution and poverty, you would have all the footmen of all the nobility sent to the Paper Garden to buy your book. As it stands, I've just spoken to your girl Sally and reserved purchase of every remaining copy for myself, so that I may protect the real woman behind that grandiose mask. You've been foolish."

He was not wrong, but she could very well hie to Scotland with no one the wiser if Josephine Grant was ever exposed. Her wine glass was quite empty. She examined it, a bit of the maroon color still clinging stubbornly to the sides.

"You do not intimidate me, Lennox."

"Elias, for the last time. I might think you would thank me."

"Oh, yes!" She made an exaggerated bow, flinging herself off the wall. "Thank goodness a duke came to save me! I was not managing perfectly well on my own!"

"You are uncommonly sensitive for such a social radical."

He shifted to match her eye line.

"Is it our gender difference? If I was a woman, would you react this way?" he mused. "What if it was a duchess that had purchased your inventory under the guise of concern for your person?"

"*Your* duchess?" She could not disguise the venom in her voice. Enough that he was unreasonably beautiful, enough that he was quick . . . he was still an irredeemable fop who was shopping for a mistress to supplement his aged matron of a wife.

"My duchess?" he laughed. "My duchess would never do such a thing. My duchess has not even read Austen."

"Not yet. She bought some today. And I appreciate the patronage." She spat out the sentence, and it burned on the way. She did need the money, no matter the source.

Josephine made sure she had all of her belongings safely tucked in her reticule, setting the wine glass on the ground without a thought. She even thought of herself inwardly as Josephine now. She had not thought of her upbringing for years. Still, she was sure that she knew enough about society to know that she could not play this game with a duke. Before her mother snatched her away to Scotland, she had completed all the requirements of an accomplished debutante. She could embroider, she could play the pianoforte, she retained a smattering of French, and she could waltz. She was proficient in reading aloud by a fire, and she could curtsey with the best of them. She simply never thought of it any more. She had made the decision to leave society and stuck to it. It was an unwelcome memory that the duke had brought with him, a phantom behind his back all the time.

"You are a classically trained pianist. That book was written by an educated woman. Yet, you are not in *Debrett's*," he said, referring to the tome that listed each member of the peerage. "How would one find out which guardian to inform that his charge was spending her nights in an establishment full of Cyprians?"

"Is that a threat?" she scoffed. She felt like her old self then, facing him fully instead of scurrying away like a scared mouse. The nobility never took you seriously if you shirked. Even her irredeemable father would not come out of a confrontation with his head down. "I am long past guardianship."

"It is just a question."

He may as well have shrugged instead of spoken.

"My father was titled, but my debut was never a priority. My parents were living separately by the time I was seventeen. My mother and I spent some time in Scotland." She decided she would not lie. This serious man had become even more serious, and he was already digging around too much. It would also not do to give him too much information, so she walked a fine line in satisfying his curiosity. "She died when I was twenty, he when I was twenty-two, and I found out that the Paper Garden was the only thing available to me from my father's holdings. I am now twenty-seven, a spinster bookseller. I could not be a governess; I was never good with children. I long ago abandoned hope of an advantageous marriage, on the shelf, as they say. Enough biographical information for you?"

"No siblings?"

"Good night, Lennox." She was able to control rolling her eyes, but it was a powerful instinct. "Forgive me if I do not thank you for forcing me to use what little money I have to publish a second edition of my book."

"My purchase should pay for that; I made sure of it."

"You speak like a businessman," she sneered. "It is very unbecoming."

Her hand involuntarily flew to her mouth. Impertinent. She could almost hear her father chasten her for it.

"I am sorry, Your Grace."

He had closed down. "Duke is serviceable. I think we understand each other. We needn't stand on ceremony, Miss Grant."

She nodded because there were no words.

"If you intend to continue doing what you are doing, you might be smarter about it."

Another nod.

She turned to go back, but found that he was following behind her. She put up a hand to stop him.

"At least allow me the dignity of returning as I left. By myself."

❖   ❖   ❖

Elias found that he liked being insulted. It happened so little that it was refreshing to be addressed by someone who wasn't shrinking away or flirting with his family name and money.

After waiting in the rotted courtyard to a count of three hundred, Elias emerged to find a flushed Nicholas waiting in the lobby. There was no sign of the bluestocking.

"Allow me a night at Ashworth?" his friend grinned sleepily. "I can smell her on my skin, and I have no intention of bathing or having this coat cleaned until the morning. My mother has been haunting the hallways late at our estate and my elder brother has returned to visit. They will know in a moment that I am in love."

"Get a hold of yourself, man," Elias said as much to himself as to Nicholas.

Dryden waited in the outer barroom and a rented hackney waited outside.

"What will you tell *your* mother?" Nicholas asked as the steadfast valet closed the carriage door.

"Hmm?"

"What will you tell your mother when word gets back to her that you follow a courtesan around like a trained pup?" Nicholas grinned.

Elias's expression did not change to match his feelings. "I am a grown man, Nicholas."

"Presumably," he snorted.

"What are your intentions with Crimson?" Elias asked, deftly turning the conversation back to his companion. "You must know that she will begin to expect something more."

"I am grooming her for my mistress, is that not obvious?"

"You said you loved her."

"Lennox," Nicholas laughed, "I will be a marquess. It's not as if I can marry the girl."

"And if she refuses a position as your *chère amie*? If she does not want you to marry another?"

Nicholas pointed his eyes in accusation.

"You are very interested in Sally's welfare suddenly. Are you not considering the same thing with the bluestocking?"

Though he was not conscious of it when the questions were coming out of his mouth, it was true, he *was* now interested in Sally's welfare. He would not have thought about it much before reading Josephine's cursed book. Josephine had put a needling statement into his mind, too: "If oppressors just instinctively realized their mistakes and felt empathy, there would be no oppression. This is why voices are needed. " He remembered the damn introduction word for word, the harridan.

"There is nothing between us." When Nicholas didn't answer, he went on. "She is addlepated and irresponsible. It is amazing she has not gotten herself killed or jailed by now. That aside, the bluestocking is not a puzzle for me to solve." Even as he spoke the words aloud, they rang untrue. "She holds me in disdain, as she plainly announced to the whole room when she cut me. I needn't muck around in a brothel to find a willing woman, and I have more important things to do, regardless."

All the same, he should send a note tomorrow along with the bill of sale from her books, something to put an end point on the whole misunderstanding.

"Not that she isn't tempting," he amended aloud. "Quite the opposite. Perhaps that's part of the problem. I have thought of little else since I met her. She does not shrink in conversation; she extends that regal neck as if we were in court, not a whorehouse. She refuses to listen to reason, even when I am endeavoring to protect her. She has a most vexing collarbone. Should I have noticed that? I keep forgetting that she is not a lady. I saw her smoke, Nic, smoke! She drank her wine in two gulps. She belongs in Bedlam where she can't cause any trouble. Or maybe I do. Do I sound mad, Nic?"

Nicholas was asleep, openmouthed, against the window. He had to be carried into Ashworth and Elias was deeply jealous of him.

CHAPTER FOUR

"The D. of L., known as the Uncatchable, has reportedly himself caught a bluebird at the infamous S.D. The ladies will be relieved to know that he is not made of stone."
—FROM A LONDON SCANDAL SHEET, MARCH 1832

Josephine stared into her morning coffee. Thank goodness she had told Mother that she had family business that would take her away from the Dove for a few nights. She needed the time to get her head together. The duke had turned her life on its end in a day's time; like Napoleon's ranks against Wellington, she could not sustain further damage. It was time to retreat and regroup.

Sally opened the front door just a hair, trying to sneak into the store. The bells announced her with a twinkle, which Josephine would have missed if she hadn't been sitting right there. She put down her paper.

"Good morning, Sally."

She started. "Mornin', Josie."

"About the sale of my books."

"Yes."

Josephine had not acted the manager much with Sally, because she had known her before "hiring" her and housing her at the Paper Garden. Sally worked harder than anyone, so Josephine never needed to reprimand her.

"He approached me soon after the show. I told him you'd be right angry," Sally said earnestly, setting her reticule on the counter. "He's persuasive." She paused, quirking an eyebrow. "And a little grating."

"You should have told him that under no circumstances would you be able to approve of the sale of the whole stock of books. I cannot undo this; you have entered into a legal contract with the duke, on my behalf. I know you did not mean harm, but this is a grave situation. You are aware that our funds are beyond limited. I cannot print more. It nearly bankrupted us the first time. It was a silly idea from the start."

Sally sat down beside her, slumping.

"I am sorry, Josie. I realized at once what I did, once he left. He's like a fog, isn't he? Says things that make you think everything will be all right."

Damnation, that he does, Josephine thought.

"It is no excuse," she said. She put her coffee down with what she hoped was an air of authority, though inside she felt terrible. "You are not to speak with him. If he returns, tell him that if he has legitimate business, he can conduct it through my solicitor."

"I'll . . . I'll pay for them somehow."

"Sally. You very well will not. I am not angry . . . I just cannot have this go any further. This man is a duke. He is not a random man on Fleet Street."

"I understand." Sally relaxed. "I really do, Josie. Thank you."

"Good, wonderful, we will complete the transaction and that will be that. Good-bye, Duke."

The words "good-bye" and "duke" were bisected by the jingle of the door bells.

This was no customer. This was an elegantly dressed footman with white hair, no wig. He looked wooden and immovable, and he did not offer a greeting. He stepped in, looked around, and walked toward the two silent ladies once his eyes found them in the room overstuffed with books.

"Miss," he nodded to Sally. The same to Josephine.

He handed her a crisp envelope.

"The Duke of Lennox." He bowed.

Josephine nodded mutely. She wracked her brain: Was there some social convention with footmen that she was forgetting?

"Good day to you both," he said pleasantly.

The bells again, then more silence. The envelope sat in front of them.

"I'll . . . continue alphabetizing the essays," Sally said. She backed away from Josephine as if she was possibly infected with plague.

The envelope sat there for another full minute while Josephine stared at it. It was not addressed to her, just a thick ivory rectangle. It was better paper than some of her most valuable manuscripts were printed on. Though it had no eyes with which to stare back, it was making a good show of it.

She broke the wax seal with the duke's crest on it, imagining that she was actually flicking him in his infernal, beak-like nose.

One piece of paper, a simple bill of sale, drawn up through his solicitor. She did not recognize the name of his man of business, of course. She would have no dealing with the rank of man he represented. It stated that the duke had verbally agreed the day before to purchase the whole stock of *On Society's Ills and the Real Price of Prostitution*, the price, and that a carriage would pick them up at her convenience. At the bottom, a scrawl read "Please accept the duke's personal thanks in the enclosed letter."

There was another smaller sheet, folded and again wax sealed.

She turned it over a few times, seeing that the ink did not seep through the back. Quality, all quality. It was wearisome. She needed to find a flaw with him, outside of the fact that he was a married man who frequented a brothel. She wished that his outside appearance reflected the wretched man he was inside.

It would not do to delay the inevitable, so she opened it.

Miss Grant, it read. *If you take issue with me addressing you in this way, you are free to burn this letter after you have read it. The price of the books in addition to your commission will more than pay for another run, if that is what you wish to do. I regret that we entered into this situation. If you would be so kind as to sign one edition for my collection, I would call it even. Respectfully yours &c, Lennox.*

Call it even! He was one for calling it even, if she kowtowed to his will. Why did he think that he had done nothing wrong? What gave him the right to meddle in her life at all? Did he think that no one would ever argue with him, that he was unimpeachable?

She grabbed the nearest copy of her book, every copy of which Sally had stacked neatly in a box near the front counter. There were quills everywhere to suit her purpose. She had one in her hand, in fact. She scribbled in anger before she really processed her thoughts.

Josephine slammed down the book and walked away.

◆　◆　◆

Later that afternoon, a letter of acknowledgement arrived at Ashworth Hall, directing Elias to send someone to pick up the books at any time to complete the sale. It was not even signed, no sense of familiarity at all. He sent a carriage at once, in a snit, and then stood scowling at the window for twenty minutes, awaiting its return. He had wrestled over whether to go himself and finally decided no.

Nicholas was fiddling with his cuff, bored.

"Eli, chap. Come away from the window. Have a drink. You are dreadful."

"They are back," he answered, without turning around. He watched as his footmen efficiently unloaded stacks of yellow-bound tomes, piles and piles of words that he wished he'd never read. He had directed them to place the vile things in the red sitting room. He could imagine how they'd be in neat little rows, like troops, like a damned battalion in his home.

"I do not understand this," Nicholas continued, deciding to drink alone. "I do not understand it at all. You found her; she runs a shop, so you bought fifty copies of the same book?"

"Yes. That is all true. Do you not have somewhere to be?"

He started walking; Nicholas followed him down the stairs and into the receiving area.

"As a matter of fact, I do not. Your servants kindly allowed me to sleep late, which means that I missed breakfast with the family. The rest of my day would have revolved around their whims, so I just sent word with Dryden that I would be returning late."

They had arrived in the red room and there they were, just as he had imagined.

Nicholas surged forward to snatch one, but Elias was in front of him. He opened the book on the top, scanning the front. No signature. Not the next one he checked, either. He got through twelve of them before he found it, buried in a middle stack.

To a man above reproach.

—JG

Nicholas raised one of the books skeptically. "On society's ills? Have you bought a lot of radical papers from the bookshop of a whore?"

"Don't call her that," Elias snapped, shoving the signed copy into his jacket.

To a man above reproach.

What the devil did that mean? Of course it could not be something simple like "Thank you" or even something sweet as in, *I will always remember our short time together.*

Instead, *To a man above reproach.*

She couldn't be serious, because he knew it would be a lie. She didn't think him above reproach. In fact, he thought she wanted to reproach him over and over. Repeatedly and personally.

He heard Nicholas flipping pages, but hadn't the energy to explain.

"May I take one of these, Lennox?" he asked.

Elias nodded assent, preoccupied. He decided he would not call on her. He would leave it alone. He would concentrate on the estate, as he should have been doing, as if he had never set foot in the Sleeping Dove.

◆ ◆ ◆

A week passed. Josephine concentrated very hard on not thinking about the duke. By no means would she allow herself to think of him by his first name. She reminded herself on several occasions to not wonder if he had gone to the Dove looking for her. This didn't matter. She would even write it down, if it was sticking in her brain too much: little scraps of paper that said things like *Doesn't matter* and *Changes nothing*. Sometimes she would decorate them elaborately, with vines. She was thinking about translating them to cross-stitches.

She could not deny, though, that she ran to the Sleeping Dove when Mother sent word that she was needed.

When Josephine entered, it was oddly quiet. All the girls were assembled around a huge, lacquered, shining piano in the spot where her old one had been. They could have been at church, they were so still. Sapphire sat at the bench, unsure notes tinkling under her fingers as if she was afraid to play it. The men were still outside in the dining area, so the women were alone with their awe.

"BB!" Sapphire cried when she noticed her. "From the duke! It's exquisite!"

Josephine had her hands out to her sides, in a gesture that she hoped conveyed the need to stop the nonsense.

"It must be sent back," she said in an approximation of an authoritative voice, though she knew it was colored by the arresting gift in front of her. "You never should have accepted it in the first place."

"Josie, he's a duke," Sally said, close to her shoulder. She sounded shell-shocked. "We cannot ignore something like this—we would risk our incomes. And he's my Nicholas's friend. Is he all that bad?"

"Loathsome."

"He's gorgeous," Sapphire said, tilting her head in a wistful way. "He smells like heaven. I know; I was in his lap."

Mother Superior reclined at the front of the pianoforte. She wore a more serious expression than Josephine had ever seen.

"This isn't about you and your game anymore, chit," she said. "Your paramour gives a gift to the Dove and has paid over half the same amount for the private audience that you will grant him. Now."

Josephine's eyes watered with rage. He would ruin everything, the foolish, foolish man. He did not play fair.

"Absolutely not," she hissed. She had to stop herself from stomping her foot like the hundreds of tantrums she had thrown in her youth. Her father had called it "ill breeding" from her mother's side of the family. "I do not have to obey his money and his title."

Sally put a hand on her arm and said for her ears only, "But we do."

"Bugger him," she swore.

All of the ladies gasped and their heads turned toward the back door. Elias was leaning against it. His legs were crossed at the ankles, lounging, as if he were watching a play. He must have been there the entire time.

"Josephine," he drawled. The sound of the name from his mouth sent chills through her. After a week of trying not to think of him, all she had done was think about him. "I implore you to discuss this without an audience."

Mother bowed low, lifting her skirts from the filthy floor to better afford her groveling. The piano shone in the room as if it were on fire. "We are sorry, Your Grace. Your generosity is appreciated by the girls of the Dove."

"Josie," Elias said, holding out his hand this time. "Please."

The buzz of flies could be heard for lack of another sound.

"You leave me no choice," she said. She was fuming. She wanted to be alone with him just so she could scream at him. Josephine crossed the room in a few steps and did not take his outstretched hand. She was already thrown enough by his mere presence, they need not touch.

"Wise decision," he murmured, close to her ear. He stepped aside so that she could precede him into the hallway.

Of course, the first thing she did was scream at him.

◆　◆　◆

"How dare you, you blithering idiot!"

"Would you rather go to the room your employer set aside for us or perhaps your courtyard?"

Elias had planned his attack carefully, based on her previous behavior. She would be righteously angry, he knew. The route that he had decided on dictated that he would just ignore her rage as best he could. He had believed it might work . . . until he saw her flashing blue eyes roll over into a menacing grey.

"You called me by my name! In front of Mother! Did you just assume she knew my name? You are very good at assuming things. What gives you the right to meddle in my life in the first place? Do you bound about London from whim to whim?"

Elias began walking down the hallway. This was a trick he used often, with much success. People will follow you if they want to continue a conversation or, in Josephine's case, if they want to bellow at you. He revised his tactic to letting her run out of steam. She eventually had to say all she had to say, hadn't she? Besides, it was good to just hear her voice.

"Oh, this silent I-am-walking-away thing will not work, Lennox. I know what you are doing. This hallway ends soon and I will not go into one of these rooms with you. I am not going to be your mistress. And take back your blasted piano."

They reached the end of the hallway, next to the room Mother had given him with her compliments, the so-called Grande Suite.

"It is not a gift for you," he told her, which was not true. He had spent the week going over all of his accounts to the farthing, making sure that any properties he was responsible for could sustain themselves, rooting out debts his father had tried to hide. He had worked straight through two nights without even realizing it, trying to keep her out of his mind. When he found a large accounting error and a surplus of money, he spent a good amount of it on getting her alone. It burned him to do it like that, but there was no other way.

He had his hand on the doorknob. "It is not just for you. It is for the girls. They deserve better than off-key music; they deserve one thing of beauty in this wretched place. Surely you cannot disagree."

Brilliant. She could not. He opened the door.

"Fine," she sighed. "The Dove appreciates your generosity. Is there something you would like me to play this evening while you find an appropriate woman for yourself?"

He actually growled. He could not stop it.

"You push me to play the villain, so I will. I paid handsomely for your time, love. You cannot just return to the floor. Mother will agree with me. If you advertise as a commodity, you must be prepared to deliver."

"I do not—"

"Yes, yes. You charge for conversation. I paid for it. So far, you have shouted at me. So, would you prefer the room or the courtyard, Miss Grant?" He gestured inside.

"But who will play piano tonight?"

"Thackeray tells me that Sapphire has been managing, though I am sure she does not have your panache."

She flushed. "Thank you."

"You have my word; I will not take liberties. Please, come in and sit down—there are things we must thrash out before I lose my mind to them."

He ushered her in, without touching her and before she could protest again. There was wine on the table as he had requested. She sat, still suspicious, and he poured her a glass. The room was gaudy but comfortable, though the bed in the corner put thoughts into his mind that were not welcome. He felt like he had a brain fever. He had never been so tempted by a woman in his life. He wanted to snatch all the pins from her hair and let it tumble onto her shoulders. He had a feeling she would argue less if they both had on less clothing. Well, if she wanted to leave the stockings on, he supposed that would be fine. His thoughts were getting away from him again. He would not stand to be lumped in with the undesirables that she catered to every night. Elias composed himself and produced the signed copy of her book from his waistcoat and slid it across the table.

"What do you mean by 'a man above reproach'?"

She expelled a burst of laughter. "Is that what I wrote? I was so angry at you, I did not even remember."

"I am to infer that it was not a compliment."

"It is true, either way. You are a duke, which no one hesitates to remind me at every turn, therefore whatever you do cannot be wrong in the eyes of a peasant like me."

Elias was having trouble reconciling the vitriol with the perfect mouth it came out of out.

"No one, outside of the members of my own family, would ever have the gall to speak to me the way you do," he said, hoping his voice was even enough to fool her into thinking he was calm.

"Does your wife?"

He had been about to take a sip of wine. Thankfully, he had not. He would have choked on it.

"My what?"

"Your wife. The one you brought to my store. She is well past childbearing age, are you not concerned with siring an heir?"

"Gads, Josie, you have—"

"Please do not explain." She grabbed the bottle of wine from him and refilled her glass, promptly drained it, and refilled it again. Perhaps she would be more logical when she was drunk, Elias thought, because she certainly could spew nonsense when she was sober. "I have narrowed it down to two possibilities: you have gambling debts and she is wealthy or she was your governess and you never truly grew up."

He put his head in his hands to stifle his amusement, but his shoulders still shook.

"Are you . . . laughing at me?" she demanded.

"Josephine," he said, muffled into his hands, unable to stop the peals from escaping, "that is my mother."

❖   ❖   ❖

Well, he was not quite as depraved as she thought. That was unfortunate, as it had been easier to resist his kindness and good looks when she had the accusation of cheating husband to level. Elias took his hands away from his face, but he was still grinning. His profile, already striking when aloof, was absolutely blinding when amused.

"I am glad I could entertain you," she muttered. She had drunk too much wine too quickly and wanted him to go away. She never should have come in the first place. He was too complicated.

"Come now," he teased. "You must see how ridiculous that is."

"I feel very silly."

"Not at all. It is very interesting to watch you run out of reasons to hate me." He gave her a smile that had to be a cultivated one, calming at the same time it was mischievous. What was wrong with this man? Why did he give her the slightest notice, much less chase her? She willed herself to concentrate his words.

"My mother would love to take up the mantle of dowager duchess, but she has found me difficult to marry off. It is the current occupation of the patronesses of the beau monde to throw ladies in front of me. You might say that I am something of a cause for them. It is mortifying. They call me 'the Uncatchable.' They are determined to find a suitable wife."

"What is wrong with them?" Her voice came out far more quiet than she wanted. "The ladies, I mean? The ones they throw in front of you?"

"Vapid. Vain. Incurious." He loosened his cravat, pulling the ends until it was a scrap of crisply folded linen hanging loose from his neck. The creases were so deep, it must have taken his valet ages. He could not have managed that artistry on his own. "Stuffy. Boring. Pie-faced."

"Your standards are a touch high, Elias. Women of their rank are raised with these qualities as their ultimate aims."

She knew. They had tried to do the same to her, to turn her into a docile and obedient cow.

"Where do they raise the women like you?"

If he continued to be likable, she did not think she could bear it. His wine glass was empty, so he began drinking out of the bottle. It was too casual. She could not be like this with a duke. There was no way it could end well.

"I am sorry," she said tentatively. "I do think we have gotten too personal. It is not within the realm of what I do at the Dove to divulge my personal history. As you said to me before, I do have to be careful if I want to continue doing what I'm doing."

"That is another thing we need to talk about," he said, stern. "I have had a week to think about what happened between us. I was curious as to why you are so secretive—yet you publish under your own name. I used every means of research available to me, but I cannot find record of you. You are educated beyond your apparent means and you say a bookshop is all you have since your father's death. Yet, there is no Josephine Grant, except on the mortgage of the Paper Garden."

She went cold, to the tips of her fingers. He could not stop meddling and he would reduce to rubble everything she worked to build.

"This leads me to believe," he continued, "that you are not who you say are."

Josephine walked to the window, thick gold curtains blocking any view of the street. She thought perhaps if she did not look at him at all, it might be easier. She ran a hand down the curtain, releasing some dust into the air. The place was filthy. Mother only did the minimal amount of required cleaning, or to be precise, the girls did. The horrible woman did not want the expense of hiring servants.

"Why do you care?" she asked.

When she moved, he moved. He was like a blasted fly. He stood too close behind her, enough that his voice was a vibration on her skin.

"I do not know. Reasonably, I do not know. Your book got stuck in my mind. It was the first time that a woman had made me think, with the exception of my little sister and my mother. You know that I spend the majority of my time mired in my father's estate. The rest of my time I spend staring at fripperies in ballrooms, bored straight out of my skull. I suppose you are exciting."

"You said you would not take liberties."

"I will keep that promise." Why could she hear his smile? That was absurd. "But. It is not a liberty if you desire it . . . do you want me to kiss you, whoever you are?"

There was no way she could turn around, though every nerve in her body wanted to do so, jumping.

"Lennox, please. Leave it alone."

"You are avoiding the question." He consulted his pocket watch. "It is only nine o'clock. I would say that I have you until at least ten."

"The question?"

"It is a shame you will not turn around and look at me. The question—which I am certain you remember—was do you want me to kiss you?"

"I cannot."

"That is answer enough. Disallowing something does not equate with not wanting it."

Josephine decided to give it one last shot, to try to drive him away.

"Your Grace, you have been rooting around in my life, but you know nothing about it. I appreciate your concern and I will even apologize for treating you more poorly than you deserved. The simple fact is that I cannot sate your curiosity or your desire."

When she was met with no response, she turned around. He was examining her with a sober expression.

"I think you are far too harsh on yourself," he said. "You do not allow much pleasure in your life. I understand this intimately, as I am guilty of the same. For one moment can we just forget that I am a duke? Forget that you have crushing responsibilities, both here and at your store?"

She steeled herself and regarded his amber eyes, now glazed over with an odd heat. She clasped her hands in front of her, then unclasped them. She wanted the moment he spoke of, before he had to return to his world and marry a respectable woman. Since he was unmarried and so was she, what harm could one kiss do? She wanted to not worry about the world for one moment, to just know the reality of his lips.

"I am trying to be a gentleman, but you make it tricky. Say yes. Say yes and stop thinking for one blasted minute."

She could not believe she was nodding, but indeed she was, one slow tip of her head, down and up again.

"Yes," she said in a barely perceptible voice. "Yes, Elias."

◆　　◆　　◆

As soon as she breathed that sweet yes, he had her in his arms. Even though he told himself otherwise, this had been his aim for the evening. He attempted caution as he put his mouth to hers and his arms around her waist. It was the easiest thing in the world to take her into his arms, as if he had been born knowing how to do it. To his surprise, she deepened the kiss, weaving both of her hands into his hair. It sent sensations all down his arms.

He groaned against her lips, his eyebrows drawing together with the ache he felt. He would have to guard that he did not let his starved imagination rule him. He could not believe he'd made it this far in swaying her, and he did not dare scare her away now. The problem was that she made staying in control a herculean task.

"One kiss," she said heavily.

"No," he said into her ear, placing another kiss against her earlobe. She shuddered, which was delicious to him. "A few kisses, once."

Josephine pulled him back up to her face and tilted her head to afford a better angle. She embraced him again with her hands clutching the ends of his hopelessly wrinkled cravat, tasting of wine. Her reciprocation increased his need and he backed her against the wall. He put his hands on it to keep them from roaming wildly over her body and kissed a trail down her neck to her astonishing collarbone.

"Doesn't matter," she said, dimly. She seemed to be talking to herself. "Changes nothing."

"Shhh," he scolded, pressing his nose to the valley of her throat, senses filled.

This time when he took her mouth, he bit her bottom lip in a soft experiment. She parted for him and his hands shot to the sides of her face as if it was an anchor. He felt her hands curl into the back of his coat and she moved against him, beginning to squirm. He thought he might be undone, then. He moved back, a shift that was torture, and it broke the spell.

"We should . . ." she said, not finishing the thought.

They were both breathless, faces still mere inches away from each other. Elias could not stop staring at her, for his part. Most of the pins had fallen out of her hair and the image was a fulfillment of daydreams he had indulged in the week away from her.

"You must let go," she said, putting her forehead against his. A lock of hair fell against his cheek, silky and scented. Her arms, tight around his back, contradicted her words.

"So must you," he replied, stealing another slow kiss. He was not sure that she would ever let him do it again, so he lingered, hoping for a strong sensory memory. After a moment, she pushed on his lapels, easing him off. She brushed her lips against his cheek as a farewell, a tender gesture that only made the parting worse.

His hypothesis had been correct. He had tested it and repeated the results, so it was true. He had feelings for the damned woman. He would not be able to leave her to her own devices, which though brave, would lead to devastation or Newgate Prison. He had feelings for this woman, whom he had met under an alias, found under an assumed name, whose real name was still outstanding.

She was fussing with her gown, peeking in the looking glass at her coiffure.

"Look what you have done, Lennox."

"I deserve reproach," he bowed.

"That you do. And so, since no one else seems to be fulfilling that task, I will." She took his hand. "I thank you for your concern and I think you may be a good man, but I can never be your mistress. If you could not guess my reasons already, you have read them in my book."

"I agree with you, not-Josephine, so do not operate under that impression that we are at odds philosophically. It is fortunate that I do, for I have forty-eight copies of the book in my foyer. I never asked you to be my mistress, if you recall." He ran a thumb back and forth on her palm, cursing the nod to propriety she observed by always wearing gloves. "My attraction to you is obvious and mutual. We can ignore that as long as you like. I cannot ignore that you are placing yourself in danger every night."

"Thank you, Your Grace, but this must end here." She took her hand away.

"Do not 'Your Grace' me, not after what just happened. May I call on you later this week? Perhaps bring Thackeray and my sister to browse the Paper Garden? Neither of them are a threat to you."

"That is not a good idea, I am afraid. It must be late now; I need to go." She eased around him with as wide a berth as she could manage without seeming impolite. She curtseyed, another practiced skill, more indication that she had the upbringing of a peer. A simple curtsey was made so much more salacious by the costume she wore at the Sleeping Dove; he could see the graceful ball of her ankle and a tempting flash of long legs. "There are many things to be done tomorrow morning."

He had already started planning how to ascertain her true identity.

"Good night. Thank you for the lovely gift to the girls. Thank you for everything . . . Elias."

Again she was gone. A maddening habit, he thought.

◆　◆　◆

Josephine stalked out of the room. Then, without changing into street clothes, she continued on straight out of the building, into a carriage, and back to her home, where she stayed in her room for a day and a half. Sally brought her food. Josephine maintained that she was sick and her wise friend did not press her with questions. Another girl from the Sleeping Dove filled in at the shop, paid out of rapidly dwindling funds.

She paced, she tried to read and failed. She played piano. She did not linger on the way his body had felt against hers, the tense energy of his form wrapped around her own. She did not close her eyes and imagine herself back in that moment when she could forget everything except his arms around her, muscles tight against his waistcoat. What she actually did was sort through the overflow of inventory that had amassed in her living quarters. Alphabetical by author, she stacked them around her bed, A to Z in a semicircle. The "S" section was very high, as were "M" and "L." One of the "A's," most unfortunately, was a certain Lord Elias Addison, not a duke at the time, but using his father's courtesy title, a series of essays on Wordsworth, De Quincey, Keats, and an odd rambling rant against foxhunting that he had apparently written while at university. She read it, of course. It was passable.

He would not come without sending word, she surmised, certainly not. That would be rude. It was almost two days now with no communication, but she could not feel safe. She paced, throwing an occasional glare at his book. Pompous essays, grandstanding, so sure of his expertise, made even more maddening because he was actually right about everything. It was galling.

On the morning of the third day, Sally knocked softly.

"Josie? Perhaps I should send for the doctor."

"No, thank you. It is just a sniffle. Not too close, dear, I do not want it spreading."

She came into the room a bit more, her hands clasped behind her back.

"Dryden. The Duke of Lennox's valet. He has been here."

She placed the same crisp envelope with the seal on the very edge of the table.

"Did you tell him I was sick?" she asked, her eyes fixed on the dratted paper.

"He did not ask to see you. Just gave me this."

"Thank you," she nodded. "You should take a break, Sally. Close the store, sit, and eat."

"Ring if you need anything," she said, backing out of the room.

She did not even wait for Sally to close the door, she tore into the envelope.

Not-Miss-Grant, it read. *If you take issue with me addressing you in this way, again, you are free to burn this letter after you have read it.*

Ye gods, he was infuriating even when he was not present.

My research is taking longer than expected, so I regret that I cannot call you by your real name, as yet.

Cad.

Finding information on the subject we discussed a few days ago has proven nettlesome. I do hate when a puzzle goes unanswered, but I am tenacious. My sources tell me that you have not been back to our meeting place. I understand this, but I do hope that you can accommodate a visit from Lord Thackeray, my sister, and I on this Thursday afternoon. I would like to talk more about your publishing ventures and my sister hopes that Sally can help her find some appropriate novels for her personal shelves. Nicholas is simply always bored. If it is agreeable that we come, you need not reply to this letter.

~~I cannot stop~~

He had left the crossed-out phrase in, instead of rewriting the letter. She thought it out of place, since he seemed so fastidious, from his frocks to his measured speech.

I have been overly occupied thinking about you. Now you surely must burn this. –L.

With much satisfaction and without a second reading, she put the end into the flame of a candle and set it in an empty bowl. Josephine watched the thing burn to ashes as she tried to decide whether or not to reply.

She kept coming back to the fact that he had said he had forty-eight copies of *On Society's Ills and the Real Price of Prostitution* in his foyer, after the wretched mistake of the kiss. Obviously, there had been one copy in the room with them. She had sent fifty, the whole lot. No one had ever bought it before. That left one book unaccounted for. Where was that book? What if it was missing? Or worse, what if it was in the hands of someone from her youth, someone from Staffordshire?

Blast it all to hell; she would have to let him call on Thursday.

Chapter Five

"If it makes you uncomfortable to think of a world of educated women, then I suggest you might instead examine your fear as a deficiency in yourself. What about an educated woman makes you feel less secure about your own person? What harm would it be for you to give the fairer sex a fair shake? What, gentlemen, are you afraid of?"

—From *On Society's Ills and the Real Price of Prostitution* by Josephine Grant

"This book is outrageous," Nicholas seethed.

Elias was shaving and he regarded his friend through the looking glass, rinsing his razor in the bowl of water beside him.

"Pardon?" He ran the razor carefully down the edge of his cheek. Dryden still tried to shave him every so often, the same way he tried to tie Eli's cravat, but it was the principle of the thing. Elias had never been completely comfortable having a valet, but Dryden had been with the family for years; he was a part of it. Thusly, Elias tried to do whatever he could with his own hands and enjoyed it. Men of leisure's brains rotted, as his favorite professor at Oxford had always told him. Elias would have taken his letter to Miss-Lady-Whomever-Grant on his own, if he wasn't so conflicted about setting eyes on her again.

"This book that you gave me, Lennox. It is shocking."

"You will have to be more specific, Nicholas." He tapped the razor again, before turning his attention to the other cheek. He probably shouldn't have let himself go two days without shaving. He was irritated, all around, and they would soon have to get in the carriage. Alessandra was very excited to go to London with her big brother. "I have 1,235 books in my library, ranging wide in era and points of origin, exactly which one are we talking about?"

"This Miss Grant tosh. The one there are fifty copies of, the lot sitting downstairs. Don't suppose you have counted them in your scholarly total yet."

Oh. Elias had forgotten that he had given the copy to his friend in the first place, and he most definitely had not expected him to read it. Nicholas did not like reading anything but the gossip pages and even then, he would rather a pretty lady read them aloud.

"You read the whole thing? I realize it is not very lengthy . . . a thesis, really, but . . . well. I am impressed, Nicholas."

"Well, not the whole thing. Enough. Enough to know that it is ridiculous."

"Do give me your criticism on the subject. I can barely contain my eagerness for your wisdom."

"The upper class is thoughtless, women, children, and poor men are slaves to them, and by God—women should be allowed to attend university?" Nicholas huffed. "You bought these books to burn them, correct?"

"I have not decided." He splashed water on his face and patted it with a cloth, then swung it over his shoulder. "Dryden, where is the duchess this afternoon?"

"Personal calls, Your Grace," he said from near the door. "The household does not expect her back until dinner."

Elias's eyes darted to Nicholas, then back to Dryden.

"I may have suggested to her that today would be a lovely day to fulfill one's social obligations," the valet added with the slightest of smiles.

"Conspirator." Elias shook his head. "I thought that my mother might give me a convenient excuse to back out of this idiotic plan."

"You are acting very strange," Nicholas said, tapping the yellow book rhythmically beside him. "You want to go see her; you do not want to see her. You say you are not thinking about her, yet you are silent all the time. You bought fifty nonsense volumes from this book-shop right after you spent weeks telling me that your finances were hopelessly botched."

"It is not as bad as I thought," Elias said, shrugging into the over-coat that Dryden held. "All that is left is to visit more notorious places and see that Father did not have anything outstanding that he was embarrassed to put in a ledger."

"You have gotten a lot of work done. More than in the entire past year."

"Yes, well. I needed an occupation."

The carriage ride was bumpy. Elias hated the streets of Cheapside. They were clogged and neglected. Progress and population were over-running the space itself. When they stepped onto the street, the air was thick and stifling. Alessandra, bless her heart, bounced up and down with excitement. At fifteen, the little blond girl was itching to get out into society. Part of the reason Elias was working so hard to put every-thing in order was so that he could give her a proper London debut and be assured of her future. Nothing in the streets of Cheapside, filthy and odorous, could help them with that.

The Paper Garden was dark and cool. It smelled of books and women.

Sally was at the front desk and looked up pleasantly as they entered. When she and Nicholas saw each other, they both bristled.

"Crim—" he started, moving forward.

"No," she said at the same time, scurrying toward the back. "Excuse me."

When she'd left the room, Nicholas turned to Elias. Elias stayed as still as possible. He knew he wanted to just let it unfold. His friend's eyes widened slightly, after darting to Alessandra.

"You should have warned me," he said in an undertone. "And you should not have brought your sister."

"I wanted her to meet them," Elias said, which was the simple truth.

"Are they not going to greet us?" Alessandra asked, her eyebrows drawn into a quizzical look that made her resemble her brother. "Was that not the Sally you spoke of?"

"You *told* her?" Nicholas demanded, sounding scandalized. It was amusing to Elias that Nicholas could ever feel scandalized.

"Of course I told her," he said, keeping his voice even. "I did not tell her . . . everything. I just told her that we both met beautiful women."

"Elias," Alessandra sighed. "I am right here."

Sally returned from the back, but she was practically hiding behind Josephine's skirt. Josephine was prepared, her head held ridiculously high. Elias smiled at her pointy nose, making a statement without a word.

She curtseyed.

"Your Grace, Lady Addison, Lord Thackeray. What a distinct pleasure."

"Miss Grant," Elias bowed his head in return. "We thank you for hosting us."

"Miss Grant!" Nicholas exclaimed, pointing a rude finger at her, taken aback. "*You* wrote that disgraceful book. The *bluestocking* wrote that book!"

"Ah," Josephine said with realization. "That's where the other copy was."

Alessandra stepped forward, employing her trademark soft smile that calmed nerves.

"You are Sally?" she said, leaning toward Sally as if she were a skittish deer. Elias always marveled at his sister's self-possession. "My brother told me you might be able to give me some recommendations of modern literature. My mother is not the most voracious reader and finds that the books I usually choose are, in her words, too advanced for me to purchase. Would you mind browsing the stacks with me? I am certain Nicholas will accompany us as well, won't you, Nic?"

Sally found her voice. "I think we may be able to introduce you to some Shelley. If you would follow me?"

The three started to the stacks together and Nicholas leaned down to Sally. He spoke with a slanted smile. "Shelley. It would figure, Sal. So sentimental."

The last things they heard were "shush" from Sally and the swish of Alessandra's muslin against stone floor as they disappeared into the shelves.

"I would have given her Byron," Josephine said, coming out from behind the desk.

"I know," he said, forcing himself to maintain a proper distance.

His plan could not be working out better: they were alone.

◆   ◆   ◆

Drat, they were alone. Josephine had hoped that she could avoid that, but once Sally and Nicholas saw each other, she knew she was foiled. The duke stood straight-backed and staid. It was impossible to look at him now without thinking of touching him. She clenched her fists in her skirts and cleared her throat.

"Ahoy," she said, stupidly.

"I did try to stay away, I'll have you know."

He was not a man who dithered.

"You let your fancy friend read my book, Lennox."

"In all honesty, I was sidetracked when he took it, and he does not usually read."

"He is angry. He will expose me."

"He is a kitten, Josie-not-Josie," Elias leaned against the front of the desk beside her and their sides exchanged warmth in the same stimulating way they had at the piano bench. "He is not a threat, and he is in love with your ward."

"She is not my ward." She stopped and turned her face toward his, too quickly. Her vision swam momentarily and then his face came into sharp focus. "He is in love with her?"

"Yes, I believe so. He is addlebrained with adoration." His keen eyes swept her face from crown to chin. Each time it seemed that he was looking at her tenderly, something inside her twisted and a crack opened in the shell that held her back. She bit her lip, anxious.

"Elias," she started, directing her gaze over his shoulder. She could not bear to look at him any longer. "I cannot afford to let this go any further. I know that society ladies are tedious to you—you, the Uncatchable—but I do not live in that world. I have more responsibility on my shoulders than those women could ever conceive of and I was not made for a dalliance with you. It is all very interesting and you are very—"

Josephine never got to finish her sentence, which she intended to end with ". . . dashing, but you must return to the ballrooms." He pulled her into him and ate her words.

When he broke the embrace, he shored her up by the shoulders. It was a gesture she had seen men do in the boxing ring, a good sport, "get on your feet" kind of thing.

"I have questions, but I cannot concentrate around you, waiting to find the next moment I can touch you. Think logically, darling, you have proven you can." He smirked and she felt a stunning mix of fury and lust. "Allow me to kiss you when I am so moved and perhaps we can actually begin to understand each other. It does not have to signify anything but the fulfillment of an urge we are both experiencing." He gave her a lazy smile. "You cannot deny you feel the same tenseness toward me."

A muscle moved in her cheek of its own accord.

"How dare you—"

He invoked the license he had given himself moments before and kissed her silent.

"Fine," she assented, pushing back from him by using leverage on his chest. "Though it is beyond improper, I will grant you that under the condition that you do not use the privilege to cut me off in conversation. It is rude."

"Duly noted." He folded his hands in front of him and reclined against a shelf, throwing his shadow over the spines of the books in the midafternoon sun. "I can be satiated for a while. Now, I would like to know what the hell I am supposed to call you."

"I thought you were playing detective."

"In the meantime?"

She tried to lean in in the same casual manner as he, but when she put her hand on the desk, it hit one of her notes. It was one of dozens of her "*doesn't matter*" notes.

"Josie will suffice here, BB or Blue at the Dove. I am used to it."

An imperial eyebrow shot up. "That—is as close to an admission as I think I will get."

She pursed her lips in a playful way. Horrified, she became aware that she was very guilty of advancing their repartee. She rearranged her features to a placid innocence. "I confirmed or denied nothing, you will find."

"Will you come back to the Dove, as a favor to me? You can play piano, we will be in public, and I will continue to keep up appearances. I will not betray your confidence—or Sally's—but being seen with me will keep you safe. Correct?"

He was too perceptive.

"Everyone will think I am your mistress," she reasoned.

"Indeed. You know very well that is normal." He got up and returned to her side. "I am thirty-one and have recently come into title. I should have damn well had a mistress for years now. They talk because I do not. If the men in the Dove thought that I was keeping you, it would be beneficial to us both. You will be safe; I will look like I'm not a misanthrope."

"I find myself unable to argue with your logic." She winced. "It is sickening."

That arm around her waist was beginning to feel comfortable and right. She would resist it. She wanted to break his gaze, but it was impossible when his eyes locked. The scrap of paper was crumpled in her hand.

"Do not swoon," he intoned histrionically.

Footsteps. They both heard them.

"Your attendants approach," she said.

"You will come tonight?" He placed a chaste kiss on her cheek and then smoothed his hair, which was a hopeless gesture that she found horribly endearing.

"Yes."

"Thank you, Josie."

"Be careful," she said, though she had no idea why.

Alessandra had chosen books and Josephine settled with her numbly. She assumed she adhered to utmost politeness, but had no memory of what she said to the young lady. Nicholas and Sally stole glances without words, both blushing and smitten. Everyone exchanged pleasantries and then the door closed again, leaving Josephine befuddled as to how to process all of it.

◆　◆　◆

Elias was euphoric as they climbed back into the carriage. He had not dared hope she would agree with him, so this outcome was nothing short of a miracle.

Alessandra showed him her books. They had chosen *Queen Mab*, with notes, and three Shakespeare plays she needed to complete her collection. He chose not to tell her that she could have borrowed any of the four from his own library, as she was so delightfully excited.

"I did enjoy Sally's company immensely," she beamed. "There are not many young women around Ashworth, Eli. It is a distinct deficit. I only regret that I did not get to talk to Miss Grant. What did you say her book was about?"

"Adult things, Allie," Nicholas said snappily. "None of your concern. Before we gush further about the pleasant afternoon, Lennox, it is unfair that you blindsided me."

"You would not have come otherwise."

"Well. It worked out in the end, lucky for you. Sally and I are going to the theatre this evening."

Alessandra lit up. "How romantic!"

"Nicholas, that is not wise," Elias scowled. "What if you are seen? Your mother will become hysteric."

"Oh, Lennox, I am not an idiot. We will go somewhere where we will not be recognized."

Whatever Thackeray did was none of his business, Elias decided. He was going to the Sleeping Dove to play piano with the bewildering woman and he was thrilled. It was unlike any other courtship he had been forced to endure or pretend. He turned to find Alessandra smiling at him.

"Dear brother, you are grinning."

"I suppose I am, dear sister."

The rest of the carriage ride home was uneventful. Elias found them the most blissful moments he had passed since . . . well, since perhaps Oxford. He might have stayed at university and worked his way up in the ranks, an ambition he never would have mentioned to the elder Duke of Lennox, were it not for the fact that his father became ill and he had to prepare to take up a dukedom. He had not thought about that possibility at all, until it happened and his life was rearranged. Now he had to think of taking a seat in the House of Lords, debuting Alessandra, and becoming head of the household. He was not the sort of man who felt comfortable wearing a coronet.

In the dark of the night, every night, he doubted that it would all be achievable. Josephine made him feel like it might work, if she were beside him.

He felt that triumphant surge until exactly the moment that he saw his mother standing on the staircase. He handed a footman his coat and bowed his head to her.

"Duchess."

"Where have you three been?"

"Shopping!" Alessandra said brightly. Elias noticed that she held up the packages from the milliner they visited earlier, but not the package from the bookshop. It was quite clever of her. "I am positively starved to get a preview of my debut, and I almost never get to see the city proper. Surely you cannot be cross about that, Mama?"

"It was very sweet of Elias to take time out of his schedule to accompany you." The duchess appraised him and he could tell it took all her effort to not fuss over the state of his clothing or hair.

"Everything is in order, Mother. I have a little time to spare."

"You are attending Lady Graham's ball tomorrow, are you not? It would be very poor form indeed to miss it and a certain Miss Francis has been asking after you."

Elias held in a sigh. The certain Miss Francis was the frontrunner for his affections, according to everyone else but him. She was a fantastically moneyed heiress, exceedingly uninspiring, and for all intents and purposes, a "perfect match."

"Yes, Mother. Nicholas and I both plan to fulfill our gentlemanly duties."

He felt Nicholas step on his foot with just enough pressure to pinch.

"I must dress for dinner," Alessandra said, yanking off her bonnet. She was still flush from excitement. Her governess was not much for adventure, so she did not get out as much as she deserved, at least not without the severe duchess at her side.

"Smashing idea," Elias agreed, brushing past his mother on the stairs.

"I read the scandal sheets, Elias," she said, after Alessandra was out of earshot. "It is acceptable for you to keep a woman one might find at an establishment like the Sleeping Dove, but do not deviate from finding a duchess."

The woman did not mince words.

"Indeed," he nodded.

"Keep to your plan, my son," she said as he passed.

He did not turn, could not—he was smiling.

"Oh, I will."

❖   ❖   ❖

Josephine had never felt so exposed by her costume at the Dove than she felt as she paced the length of the dazzling piano the duke had given the establishment. Her thoughts were getting wildly out of control and her hair had suffered for it—it was piled on her head in a slapdash manner, not entirely fastened by pins. The crowd was just starting to stream in. She had tried to keep to herself, which the girls had kindly respected. They knew that she was fragile. It was an embarrassing emotion she had rather not display to them—they depended on her. This game she and the duke were playing was so ill-advised. She knew she was giving into flirtation, against all of her better judgment.

The line of leering, half-drunk men filled the room. Some made their approach to their chosen ladies straightaway. A large portion of the girls had regulars, some had more than one. She did not see the duke among them. She had not entertained the fact that he would not come.

Just as she was about to retreat to the courtyard in mortification, a glass of wine appeared at the crook of her arm. She turned to see Elias's masked face, his mouth crooked with amusement.

"Are you looking for me, lovely?"

"How did you manage to not only sneak in without my notice, but also get me a glass of wine in this short amount of time?"

"And sherry for myself. I am an honored guest now. I want to wink at you, Josie, but I will not. I have made arrangements with Mother for payment, as I promised to keep up appearances. You will get a fair amount for your time, I assure you."

"A man above reproach, indeed," she said. "Won't you sit down, Your Grace?"

"After you," he bowed.

Once they were settled and Josephine was warming up her hands, she spoke more freely.

"Do you think we will end up in the gossip pages?"

"Again? We already were and I kept that paper. I intend to have it framed." He took a drink to stifle his smile, but she could see it all the same. "If we would become a consistent item in those pages, society would only identify me. They might call you BB. They would only ever mention 'a gentleman's club' or the ridiculously see-through initial system they favor."

"I am worried about Nicholas and Sally, are you not?"

"Somewhat." He curled his leg around hers, under the piano, hidden by the shimmering gold curtains that surrounded it. His boot rubbed against her stocking, startlingly stimulating. "Hmm. *That* is inspiring. I may find ways to tempt you even here, without being able to invoke my kissing clause."

"You should tell me more about yourself," she deflected. "I only know what I have been able to find through the taradiddle."

"That would bring me no closer to my goal of finding out your identity." He scratched his face under the mask. "I hate this thing."

"I prefer you without it, as well."

Josephine, shocked and somewhat embarrassed at her own boldness, went to the anchor of the glass of wine.

"Though I cannot deny that it adds an exciting hint of mystery."

He ran the edge of his boot up her leg, the boot she knew was polished to an astonishing sheen by one of his many servants. She sucked in a breath.

"You should . . . move over. Appearances' sake, remember?"

"I thought we agreed that the appearance was that you are my mistress."

"Oh, well, yes. I suppose we did."

Elias took a bold, deliberate stare around the room, his glass of sherry near his lips.

"It is just as I had imagined it. I cannot count the pairs of eyes darting envious and furtive glances in our direction."

"I cannot believe you are putting yourself on the line like this."

"This is no shame to me, love. As I said, the gentlemen are all mad with jealousy that I have been able to land such a prize."

"Without all of the rights," she said firmly.

"That is understood," he said, his eyes scanning her neck and the rebellious tendrils of hair that refused to be held down by the traitorous pins. "That is, unless you consent to it, which I suspect you want to. I want to, most ardently."

"Lennox."

She tried to put the right note of warning in her tone and began an airy concerto as background music.

"Always scolding," he smiled next to her. "It does not work, you must have seen by now. I enjoy it."

"Then I shall have to start agreeing with you on all counts."

There was a beat of silence as he considered, then he shrugged, the tiniest lift of his refined shoulder.

"Either way, I win."

He sat and listened to her play for rather a long time, while she tried to ignore that her body was buzzing.

◆　◆　◆

As soon as Sapphire came over to give Josephine a break, Elias took her hand and hurried her back to the courtyard before she could launch a protest. He slammed the gate behind them, laughing because they had practically been running. He kissed her, deep and swift, shedding their masks in turn. They made a faint clatter as they hit the ground.

"Lennox," she said with a most fetching rasp, "we must keep our heads—wait. Did you clean up the courtyard?" She turned her head as much as she could, taking in the transition—the courtyard was no longer a dank and dark place. He followed her neck as it craned, kissing along every inch that she exposed to his reach.

"I had it begun, yes," he said, lifting her hand to his mouth and peeling off her glove. "Truly, Josephine, I am too distracted to converse and you need to honor our agreement."

"I feel different in this outfit now," she said hoarsely as he yanked off her other glove. Her hands went inside his coat and she contained a snarl when she ran them up his chest. "It feels indecent."

"Just touch me, Josie. Please, be quiet for a godforsaken moment."

Blessedly, she complied and her bare hands touched his face as she brought it to hers. He was lost for a few minutes, his hands wandering to the sides of her waist, currently under too many layers of fabric and sequins for his taste. She leaned into him, his back against the newly dirt-free stone walls, no longer covered in rotting vines. He smiled into her kiss—restoring the courtyard had been one of his better ideas.

Every wandering thought was obliterated when she raised her leg against him. He dragged his hand down her stocking and groaned against her lips.

"Stop, Josephine," he heard himself say. He applauded his real-world self, the self that was not kissing her, on his restraint. The one that was kissing her, the ethereal, wispy Lennox, was too surrounded by her essence to even speak.

"But I am still distracted," she teased. "You are far too used to being the word of authority. You must remember this is an agreement with two sides."

If he was not on the verge of losing control before, he was when he felt her tongue on his ear. His hands cupped her bottom of their own accord and crushed her to him.

"Vixen," he rumbled, biting her bottom lip. He throbbed against her and he knew he had to disentangle before he completely lost command of his senses. As much as he wanted to, he could not ravish her here. He planted a last kiss on her nose and released her leg from its grip by delicately unhinging her ankle from his thigh, her well-formed, neatly comported ankle . . .

"Gads, woman," he sighed, picking up the pins that had fallen from her hair. "Sit."

He gestured to the table he had requested be put in the corner, where fresh flowers had replaced the corpses of the old ones and the wood of the chairs was no longer suspect to break if one put weight on it.

"Oh, Eli," she said, caught off guard. Her hair was worse off than before, but the candles on the table lit her like she was something celestial. The wisps around her head formed a halo to complement the delight on her face. "This is . . . too, too much."

"You are a wreck," he chided, setting her down in the chair and standing behind it. "Let me see what we can do about this hair."

It would be a shame to waste an opportunity to get so close to her graceful neck.

"When should we go back?" Josephine asked softly, as he ran a pin up her neck to capture a curl and twist it.

"Half of an hour?" He traced that superb collarbone, sweeping the stray strands to the back of her neck. "Whenever we want? Never?"

She sighed with contentment and it was like music to him. It pained him to think that kind of a sigh was few and far between for her. She nestled her head against his rumpled waistcoat, a shatteringly affectionate gesture, and he curled his arm around her. There was the night air, and their breathing, and nothing at all was wrong.

"You are cruel," she said into the holy silence. "When you go away, it will be so much worse, even worse than it was before."

"I remind you that we have scarcely known each other for a fortnight. You have no evidence to support me suddenly turning tail and running. What have I done that you will not give me the benefit of the doubt?" Elias turned her alluring face up to him. He felt he needed to make her look—perhaps it would be harder for her to ignore his words or misinterpret. He also selfishly wanted to see her eyes, but it broke his heart when he saw the sheen of tears obscuring the blue. "I have followed every possible prescription you might have for a gentleman, and

I know because I read your rules. I have tried to protect you without trying to keep you. The only real charge you had against me was the repugnant fallacy that I was married to my mother. I have not stepped over any bond of propriety without explicit or implicit permission. If you will never trust me, madam, I shall be sorely displeased."

"Lennox, I knew men like you in the drawing rooms of Staffordshire, and I know enough to not get my hopes raised."

She smiled and it was a bittersweet little thing, altogether different than the catalogue of smiles he had seen in her arsenal thus far.

Staffordshire, he filed away, concurrently brushing a thumb down her cheek. *Men like me.*

"I will endure your misgivings, then, for as long as you like. I will not be going anywhere unless you tell me to disappear and truly mean it."

"I wish I could do that—and truly." She paused to wriggle from his grasp. He did not make it easy for her, but strained a bit against her as she moved away. He did not want her thinking that she was easy to let go. "But for tonight . . . yes. I need time away from you. You clog my brain. We have put on a show for the crowd, to the ends of our charade, so our mission is a success. Perhaps I will see you tomorrow evening?"

"Absolute—oh, hell." His fingers automatically went to his cravat, straightening it here and there, a nervous habit that occurred whenever he was reminded of an unpleasant social obligation. "I have to go to a ball."

"Oh," she said with a too-offhand tone. "Well, have a splendid time."

"I must go. I do not have a choice."

"I understand," she demurred. "I do, really."

"Josie . . ."

She shook her head, almost imperceptibly. "This will never work."

"I have hired a carriage for you. It will arrive approximately ten minutes after I depart."

"Thank you. You continue to do the unnecessary, Elias. I must play for a bit longer, but—you should go."

Josephine stood. They looked at each other uneasily. Whatever she was thinking, he did not know, but he was deciding if he should kiss her good night.

"Good night, my lady," he nodded.

"It was," she replied. "Sleep well."

He did not think that was in his near future.

❖　❖　❖

The carriage ride felt much longer than usual. She suspected the driver was one of Elias's footmen without livery. Damn that intrusive, exasperating man. There were so many things he deserved to know—had deserved to know before he involved himself so acutely in her life. It was quick and intense—she had thought he would disappear at every turn, ceasing to prevent a problem. Now it was too late, at least for her own chance of escaping with her heart unscathed.

She longed to hear him say her real name, her true name. The person at the still core of her wanted to know him. She wanted that passion directed to the woman she was. She acknowledged that.

She lit a fire against the chill when she got home, since Sally had not yet returned from the theatre with Nicholas. Josephine had hoped to find her safe at home, but instead she was still off gallivanting with a man who would surely break her heart. Not that Josephine had any right to lecture on heartbreak, not when the same thing was happening with the duke. She stared into the flames torpidly.

She felt consumed by him. She felt frightened. His words rang in her mind all the time, and she replayed their encounters in daydreams. She felt such a riot. She could not possibly digest the whole mess.

Sally, rosy with guilt, swept through the door.

"Don't lecture, Josie," she began, slinging her reticule onto the table merrily. "Tell me about your evening with the duke!"

"Were you seen with Thackeray? Stepping out with him was an enormous risk."

"Humorless Josie," Sally frowned, disappointed. "Are you not happy?"

"No," she grumbled. "I am not. We should be ashamed of ourselves, careless idiots. And I am tired."

"Let me ease your mind; we were not seen. But the theatre was amazing—you would not believe the spectacle. Nic wanted to be an actor, did you know that? His family frowns upon it as an ungentlemanly occupation, but I told him that he should follow his desires. He said that was good advice." She smiled distantly, as if recalling an earlier point in her night. "He is such a singular man."

"I told you when you began . . . you will regret getting carried away."

"It is too late for that," she said. "I love him. And he loves me, Josie. Would you deny us the bit of happiness that we can steal in this world?"

She had no answer. Certainly, she wanted happiness for Sally. She could not see how that could ever happen with a man who was heir to a marquess, a man who would have to cast her aside for a title and all the baggage that came with it. It was all but the same thing that her father had done to her mother. She had seen it happen over and over again. Sally, overwhelmed by the flush of first love, would hear no such thing. It was just as Josephine had feared.

"Josie," Sally said, drawing a breath. "You have been very kind to me, but it is time for another girl to take my place here at the Paper Garden. You know there are many who would be grateful for the opportunity. I will be fine and you needn't worry about me anymore."

"Is he keeping you? Has he rented you a house?"

"That seems to be where we are heading." Sally grinned sleepily. "You must admit, for a girl like me, I could have done worse for myself."

Sally Hopewell had never known either of her parents. She had grown up in orphanages. In the almost five years Josephine had run the Paper Garden, there had been fifteen other girls similar to Sally, who had come to the Garden when it was clear they were in danger of abduction by Mother's thugs. The girls came and went depending on their circumstances. It always started when Josephine noticed the suspicious nobles singling them out of attention. She would approach the girl, offer shelter without making a fuss, in exchange for help at the bookstore. Very few refused. Josephine tried to do this as discreetly as possible, not wanting Mother Superior or Digby to know where she lived or what she was trying to do. Out of the girls before Sally, ten had ended up kept, one married a tradesman, two had died, one ended up the most notorious prostitute of the decade, and one married a curate. It wasn't a terrible record, all told.

Only Sally had continued working at the Sleeping Dove after Josephine's offer of employment. She knew it was because of Nicholas, so his taking Sally as his mistress should have been no surprise. It had still taken Josephine off her guard a bit. She wasn't sure she could get used to functioning without Sally's cheerful presence.

"I wish you would be happy for me, dearest," Sally said, clasping her hand. "I am in raptures and so very thankful for your help this past year. I could have been taken away—or worse—if you hadn't opened your home to me."

The same story, over and over. The girl would be happy for a few months, and then it would begin. She would be debased and cast aside. The man in question, since he was a peer, would marry respectably and sometimes give up his mistress for the time being, in deference to his new status. When he took up again, it would be with a different, younger woman.

"I wish you the best, dear, you know this. I just know it will end badly."

"You can really be cold," Sally snapped back. "It's no wonder that cross, tiresome prude of a duke loves you."

"I am not cold, I am sensible. And the duke is not—"

Sally waved a hand dismissively. "Whatever you say. The point is he loves you."

"Pardon?" she said belatedly, since a loud tone seemed to be sounding in her head, an expanse of air between her ears that made a hollow, high-pitched whine. "You mean that he likes me? For some insensible reason, the man actually finds me amiable, that much is clear. I suppose."

Sally shook her head. She was looking at Josephine, with . . . what? Was that pity?

"Nic says Lennox never likes anyone. Love or indifference."

"You call him Nic? Oh, Sally, that is too familiar."

"Do you not call the duke Elias?"

"No, well, he . . . he forces me to . . . he is relentless, incorrigible. I do it so that he will shut up."

Sally raised an eyebrow and hugged her friend.

"We are both tired, Josie. I will tell you in the morning how Nic also said that the duke has never before dropped his studies to chase a skirt with such fervor." She kissed Josephine on the top of her head. "Good night, dear."

"Sally!" she called after her rapidly disappearing form, running up her spiral stairwell, laughter echoing all the way to the top.

CHAPTER SIX

"Is it any wonder that some of us prefer the company of scholarly papers to the cacophony of the ballroom? Who can help but be entranced by verse and cutting wit within the leaves of a good book when the rest of our lives are filled with interactions that are little beyond the prescriptions of politeness that have ruled our society since time immemorial?"

—FROM THE *COLLECTED ESSAYS OF LORD ELIAS ADDISON*, TREATISES FROM HARROW AND OXFORD

Elias felt ill at Lady Graham's ball, where he stood next to his mother and nodded and nodded and nodded. He thought his head might fall off, or split at the neck, spilling precious champagne on the dangerously polished floors, sending dancers slipping over themselves and landing in a heap. Elias was standing in a crowd of the duchess's friends, doing his duty to show his face. Miss Francis was also at his mother's side, like having been forced into the position. Just across from them, Nicholas entertained the matrons. Elias was covetous of Nicholas's ability to charm people even in mundane conversation.

Elias realized he was staring vacantly at a certain Miss Francis.

"I say, Duke," Thackeray interjected, his voice theatrical, at once charming the ladies and annoying Elias. "Have you reserved any dances with this delightful young woman yet?"

Miss Francis blinked up at him. Once, twice. Pause. Again.

"I most certainly did, Thackeray. And as I recall, you have expressed interest in her friend, Lady Sherlock?"

Nicholas scowled behind his hand at Elias. Lady Sherlock was a buck-toothed horror with a personality that far outran her visage. Her conversation was ceaseless and vulgar.

"You mistake me for Lord Blawnox," he returned.

"Good show," Elias told him in an aside, before turning to the larger group. There was always a "larger group" to turn to at these balls. "Perhaps I can get the ladies more punch?"

Miss Francis handed him her glass daintily. He wondered what she thought attractive about all the blinking she did. He could not understand it.

Refilling the glasses was merely a chance to break away from the hens, which was Elias's chief aim at balls and dances. He passed a tight gaggle of girls and heard his miserable nickname on someone's lips. He couldn't help overhearing the rest.

"Shame that such a beautiful man is such a bore," said a girl he could not identify, rigid blond ringlets crowding a cupid face.

"Have you talked to him? I tried, mark me, I did. Somehow he began to natter about papers he had written at Oxford. Shakespeare, Wollstonecraft, that horrid De Quincey, tosh. Those eyes, though. I might be able to endure it."

The girls giggled and Elias moved on, with his so-called spectacular eyes and tiresome demeanor. It was becoming a Sisyphean task. There was a spectre in his mind all the time: He saw Josephine in each dress he observed, he saw himself swirling her across the floor, he saw her raise a glass to her lips and make the horde around them laugh. She could do what he could not; she could charm them. He might be able to enjoy a dance, for once.

A hand clapped on his back and he jumped.

"Elias, my boy! It has been too long since I have seen your face."

When he turned, he could not believe his luck. He was looking at his Uncle Harrington, his mother's brother, from Staffordshire. A tiny smile of triumph crept onto his face.

"Uncle Harry, what an altogether pleasant surprise."

"I should have addressed you as duke, eh? I was too eager to see you to mind my manners."

Lord Benedict Frost, the Earl of Harrington, was one of Elias's favorite relatives, a man of good humor—a surprise, since he was the brother of the fearsome duchess. He was also the father of Elias's cousin and childhood chum, Sebastian, who would be the next earl. Naturally, Elias had been thinking about him yesterday when Josephine mentioned Staffordshire in the fog that the courtyard had thrown over her defenses. He had decided immediately to write to Uncle Harry, so this could not be more convenient.

"What brings you to London?"

"Oh, I am expected to be at every one of Lady Graham's balls. She and Lord Graham have been our dear friends for the last thirty years." He glanced around with barely masked disdain. "Regardless, I do so hate the city during the Season."

"And your lovely wife?"

"Also here. She would not miss this . . . delightful . . . soiree. I believe she has gone to seek out your mother."

"Godspeed to her. I am retrieving drinks. Walk with me?"

"A pleasure, my boy." He clapped his nephew on the back one more time. "How are you holding up being thrust into the position of patriarch?"

"I suppose I am acquitting myself. Things seem to move very fast."

"We have every faith in you, Elias. Should you need anything—I know that I am primarily in the country, but I will do anything in my power to make the transition smooth."

"Actually, Uncle," he initiated, handing the empty glasses to a servant and lowering his voice after a circumspect glance around. "I have a friend who is looking for an old acquaintance he knew around your part of the countryside. I thought either you or Sebastian might know, but your son is still in India the last that I heard. It is fortuitous that I find you here. My information is limited and I would have to ask your utmost discretion. It would have been around ten years ago that she left Staffordshire. She was the daughter of a titled man who separated from his wife when the child in question was seventeen. That might have been scandalous; in fact, I expect it would have been a huge gossip item. Does any of this sound familiar to you?"

"Hmm," Lord Harrington pondered. The servant had returned with the drinks; he bowed his head and took instant leave. "Vaguely, but a lot of what comprises gossip never reaches my ears. I cannot tolerate the pecking. I can inquire around if you wish—discreetly, of course—and see what I can find. I must ask, though, is this one of Thackeray's harebrained schemes?"

Elias laughed. "No, no. A respectable guess, however."

They wandered back toward their family, none too quick. For the Uncatchable and tedious Duke of Lennox, the excitement of the evening had already reached its zenith.

❖ ❖ ❖

Josephine closed the shop while helping Sally move into her new home, all courtesy of the debonair Lord Thackeray. When she returned home that afternoon, sweaty and exhausted from effort, Lennox was sitting inside. He was reading quietly while his valet stood in the corner, just as tall and shadowy as his master. Elias's legs were kicked up on her table, shapely in a different pair of boots than the day before, though they still brought back the image of him running one up her stockings. It was irritating that he just sat nonchalantly, as if he had any right to be there. He looked as if a speck of dirt would dare not touch him, whereas she looked as if she had been sweeping chimneys.

"What are you doing here?" she demanded, more than frazzled.

"Reading Peacock. What rot." He closed it with a snap. "Waiting for my fake mistress."

"You did not send word." She pulled off the tatty bonnet she had worn because it would not have been prudent to dress as a lady when one was a woman, a woman pushing an armoire into a more advantageous position of a room.

"I do not believe I am required to, am I, Dryden?"

"No, Your Grace," the valet replied. "Not generally . . . in these types of arrangements."

"Oh, that will never do," she protested.

"It must. It is expected that I will pay you afternoon visits. I have not brought my ducal carriage, of course. Dryden will retrieve me before dinner. It is a common occurrence, you know, darling. You wrote all about it."

"My neighbors will think . . ."

"Your neighbors will think you lucky." He widened his eyes just a touch, playful. He slid out of the chair in one smooth movement. "They will certainly respect you. I daresay, Josie, your business will improve."

"You do not realize what a bad idea this is, Your Grace."

"Stop. Calling me. That." He advanced slightly on her and she could not help moving back; it was a reflex.

"Dryden, I need to speak with Miss Grant." The duke waved his hand as a dismissal. "Please come back at five."

"Five! It is two! You cannot be here for three hours!" She was aware of her voice rising to a yelp. By the time she had gotten halfway through her disapproval, Elias's valet was gone.

"Are you going to ask me about the ball?" He was too close again and her voice had deserted her. "It was endless. All I could think of was you."

"Eli, stop," she entreated. "Drama is the last thing we need."

His nose wrinkled. "You smell awful. What have you been doing?"

"How very polite." She tried to shrink away from the handkerchief that he had produced from his pocket, but he began dabbing her face.

"Hopeless," he sighed. "You must bathe. Fortunately, I knew that no one would be able to dissuade you from manual labor with Thackeray's ladylove and I prepared for this eventuality. You'll find a hot bath upstairs."

"I think not, you rake," she muttered

"Oh, do not be missish; I shan't look. I will finish reading this ghastly book and we will talk. I told you I would take no freedoms, but for our little scheme to work it does have to look like we are enamored, which means making it look like we spend time alone."

Blast, blast, blast.

"You realize this is going too far," she admonished, brushing past him. No matter the source, she did need to bathe, and it was not often she had a hot bath in water that she had not fetched herself.

"I do," he said behind her. "Three hours alone. I must say, even I am impressed with myself. That is, unless you have some appointment that I do not know of, which I very much doubt. I tend to be rather . . ."

They had stopped just outside of her bedroom.

" . . . thorough in my research."

Josephine considered for a beat and then turned the knob on the door to her sanctuary.

Or, though she could not bear to be honest with herself, the ghost of her former self turned the knob on the door to her sanctuary.

"Very well. You will not leave me alone. Fine. My mother told me that I should wait for the most persistent bastard of a man and then give him a chance. You fit the bill. I have given you every opportunity to go away. You will have only yourself to blame." She pushed the door open, imperially awakened. "You want to become intimates? You want to talk. Fine, Elias. Come in."

◆ ◆ ◆

His self-assuredness ground to a fine powder and blew away when she started the first syllable of "very" in that monster of a voice, that commanding-a-ballroom voice. She was frightening. She was different. She was certainly not a peasant.

His first sight of her room was her bed, rumpled sheets, surrounded by stacks and stacks of books in no apparent order. Maybe alphabetical. Whatever it was, clearly only she understood it.

"What the devil are you doing with all of these books in your chamber?"

"I am putting them away. Organizing them. Exactly when else was I supposed to attend to that while you molest me, keep me out late at the Dove, and your friend takes away my shop girl?"

"There is much to attend to, yes. I will send some footmen over and . . ."

"Oh, you will not," she barked, yanking a towel from her vanity. He glanced once over at the steaming water, tendrils of heat coming off of the surface in graceful swirls, and resolved it would be the last time he would look there. "You will do no such thing. Turn around. If you go to the third book down in the 'A' stack, you will find your book of essays. Perhaps you would like to sign it for my collection? I should have known you would write portentous treatises."

"Not under 'L' for Lennox? Nonsensical. People would look for my title, if they were looking for my book. Perhaps 'A' for Addison is your logic?"

"No, Eli. It's under 'A' for ass."

He heard her shed her chemise and step into the water. Turning around would be an inexcusable breach of trust. She sounded amused, at least.

"Did you bother to read it?" he asked. "Or am I above your notice?"

"You disagree morally with foxhunting. I bet they loved that at Eton."

"I went to Harrow, actually."

"How gauche," she returned. This time he could hear the snicker in her voice.

"As if you would know anything about it," he said. "I do not suppose you had a lot of dukes visiting your part of Staffordshire?"

"Ah, you remembered."

"Remembered? I tucked it away like a gem."

"So, foxhunting and literature. A collection of essays you wrote at Cambridge?"

"Wrong again. Oxford."

"You've been all over the place, it seems," she said.

"Like Staffordshire, for instance."

The splashing of the water stopped. She was considering her words.

"Harrington probably does not remember me, Elias. He and my father were not close neighbors or even friends. I am sure they knew of each other, but not enough that he was ever a guest at my house. Having thought of it, though, I do remember your visits to the area vaguely. I was only a girl, but my father loved to watch nobles and gossip. Still, he would have had no contact with Lord Frost or his father, the earl. He was not beau monde."

"I am not sure I believe that—what title did you say your father held?"

"Sloppy," she purred. "Direct questions will never work with me. Also, you know very well that I never told you that."

"I am trying to gauge the breadth of the scandal involved in your family history, Josephine. I know I could not hope that you would just simply present me with useful clues. Furthermore, I cannot . . . concentrate."

He heard the sponge dunk in the water and tried not to think of Josephine running it over her skin. He shed his waistcoat. He suddenly couldn't stand the heat of her scented bedroom for three hours with it weighing him down.

"I can guess what you find so diverting, Eli. Distracted dukes are entitled to kisses, are they not?" she mused from behind him. "Alas, I cannot honor our agreement right now. It would be highly improper."

If she was trying to stop him from interrogating, she happened upon the only likely tactic. Elias forgot his line of questioning and could only think now of pulling her out of the water, dripping, and carrying her to the bed.

He cleared his throat.

"Quite right. It should also be noted that you do not play fair, madam."

"I believe you set the precedent for dirty strategies."

"Are you flicking water at my shirtsleeves?"

"That I am."

Aggravated, he sat on her bed with his back to her and began reading.

"Ignoring me will work," she taunted, splattering him again. "You are so very good at ignoring me."

"What the bloody hell has gotten into you?" he snapped.

He felt extremely asinine, sitting in her room like some besotted sop, letting her mock him without rebuff. She did not want his help, even if there was an attraction between them. He felt like a dupe, refraining from the feast of an image behind him. She made him sit and heel, which he had done, but she would still never trust him. It was unworkable. Even if he did find out what her story was, she would resent him for it. He wanted to dash, but it would be at least two and a half hours before his carriage returned. Spending an afternoon with

Josephine should have been easy, it sounded like a lark, but now it felt pitiful.

"Elias?"

"Hmm?" he emitted, not looking up from the words he was not reading.

"Am I boring you?"

From the shuffling, he thought she was getting out of the tub. Yes, he could hear her putting on a robe.

"Dreadfully," he replied in his best disinterested brogue.

She was standing at the foot of the bed. Surely since she was to some extent clothed, it would be an opportune time to give her a withering glance. When he attempted, he found he could no longer manage the expression on his face. He believed the romantic poets would have termed it something like "struck dumb." Josephine's legs were bare and uncovered by the robe. Her hair was only half up, tangled, frowsy. She smelled like the bath and floral soap, which wafted over the bed.

Her blue eyes glittered with something he could not identify. He was not sure he liked this change of demeanor, this aggressive assertiveness. She seemed a little too dangerous. She seemed like a bad idea. His mind was persistent in reminding him that he had no idea who she was or where she really came from. As much as it felt like they were growing closer, he knew nothing about her. He did not know what she might be capable of.

"This robe has been around since I was quite young. It does not fit as well as it used to, I am afraid. It is imported, I believe, from somewhere terribly exotic. I rarely wear it."

"That," he said from his dry throat, "is a shame."

He was at the head of the bed, clutching the book for some reason, open against his chest. She sat on the very edge of the foot of the mattress, the embroidered robe falling open at her neck, precariously open. One more shift would give him a glimpse that he barely dared imagine.

She inclined her head toward him.

"Why are you here?"

"I—complicated—"

Whatever half-arsed explanation he had been trying to come up with evaporated into thin air when he realized she was crawling up the bed, toward him.

"We are alone in my bedroom. If we cannot be honest with each other here, then we cannot at all."

Her progress had brought her right up to him, trapped him against the wall of pillows on her giant headboard. He could not help but lean into her kiss, but he was not responsible for the fact that she was straddling him. He would admit that his hands slid down her back and adjusted her, the silk of her robe against her skin making her seem malleable. He stiffened in more than one way.

"*That* is why you are here. Why you chase me." She ran a hand through his hair and across his neck, her recently scrubbed fingers still hot from the water. "Truthfully the reason you are here."

"No. I mean, yes, but not like—you mistake me."

"I do not," she said, running her hands up his chest, unburdened by the waistcoat. The book, which had still been pressed between them like a final barrier, dropped off the bed. *Good-bye, Peacock*, his unhinged brain punctuated. "If this . . . what is about to happen between us . . . is your ultimate goal, then let's have at it. I shall save you the trouble of pretending interest in my well-being."

His mind was fighting for control of his body, and his body was very close to winning the match.

"I am not pretending," he ground out, lifting her off of him.

"Are you—rejecting me?" she asked in disbelief, drawing back on her knees and not having the decency to adjust the robe.

"I am not just trying to seduce you!" Elias shot off of the bed, his voice far too loud. He could not stop it, any more than he could stop throwing his hands in the air with vexation. "I am trying to get to know you!"

Ridiculous, his brain chimed in. *You are ridiculous. You are a duke. You cannot "get to know" a female shopkeep who plays piano in a whorehouse and also houses disreputable women and writes radical papers.* His mind boggled at the list of reasons he should not pursue her. She put it into words.

"You cannot become friendly with me, or court me, which seems to be what you are doing . . . though I wonder if you are consciously aware of it. We cannot have a romantic story." She wound the ribbon that tied her robe around her finger: once, twice, thrice. He fixated on the circular movement, every muscle in his body stretched tight. "You read too much fiction if you think we can come to a resolution in the real world. The scandal would be of Byronic proportions and you, sir, are noted for your adherence to rules. I have nothing to offer you but trouble with the society you must continue to navigate all your days. You are the Uncatchable; I am unsuitable. That is all that is going on here."

"I hate that nickname."

"I laughed when Sally told me," she smiled. "It sounds as if it was invented to annoy you."

She lounged back on the pillows and pulled her robe back to a modicum of decency, which he took as an act of mercy.

"Two hours left, I suspect. I think they will be our last two hours in each other's company."

"Likely," he said, sinking back onto the bed with defeat. "I do not think you will react well to more questioning, and I will not allow you to give yourself to me in order to drive me away. Which would not work, dear lady, do you think one time would satisfy? So, what do you suggest we do for two hours?"

"Lie back, Elias. I shall behave."

She nestled against him, using his chest as a pillow.

"It has been a long few days," he sighed.

"Yes," she agreed, curling an arm around his middle and closing her eyes. "You are so very comfortable."

"As are you, but I agree that this has to stop," he said, putting his arms around her too easily. "What are we doing, love?"

"I have no idea," she yawned, nestling further under his arm.

Neither of them awoke until Dryden was at the door, ready with the slightest smirk for his tousled and sleepy master.

◆　◆　◆

Josephine made a noise of protest when Elias slid out from under her, but she could not lift her body from the miasma of the hot bath and the unrelenting warmth of his nearness. She was just so tired, and his form against her was so reassuring. He kissed her on the head and left light-footed. She thought perhaps he said something, but she was half in dream state.

When she finally did awake, her bed smelled like him, and he smelled like home. Josephine had been dreaming crazily, of a country ball like any of her youth, but he was there. He was one among the endless lines of overly self-important men, the young scholar and future duke. Elias was even worse because he was intellectually snobby, she thought, the tried and true Oxford man who bore the burden of dukedom. Even in her dream, Josephine regarded this as absolute tripe. She guessed she was eighteen or so, seeing him across a line of dancers, a face weaving in and out of view. He would have been in his early to midtwenties, in her dream-logic, perhaps visiting from university, and she encountered him when he visited his uncle. He was pompous and she watched with disdain as the other girls her age tried to court him. She whispered little invectives at him and got secretly drunk on punch. They kissed in a garden. He whispered her real name.

She shook herself awake. Her imagination had gotten away from her.

It had gone too far. She wanted to let him in.

It was a nice dream, but she reminded herself that she was just prolonging the inevitable. Purging him from her mind would be a long and taxing process, but she had enough to keep her busy. She had much to attend to that had fallen by the wayside during the sham of their fake courtship. She needed to write some letters that seemed as if they were from Scotland to preserve her now-shaky front. She needed to remember the reasons that she had left the life of the peers behind, those people and their vanity.

She lit some candles as the sun went down, but could not leave the bed. It would break the spell and she would have no choice but to return to her responsibilities.

Sally barely knocked, but breezed into the room with her eyes wide. "What in heaven's name did you do to that man?"

She was dressed in finery that must have been fresh from the shop. She looked like a lady. She removed the fancy bonnet she wore now and placed it on a side table with care. It was a sharp contrast to the clothes that she had been able to afford and the gaudy costumes of the Dove. It did Josephine's heart good to see it.

"Nothing," she lied. The better question is what she had *wanted* to do to that man, but had not.

"He tells Nic he will not be leaving the house. He sent him home and told him not to visit. Nic's very worried. He says it's not at all like the duke. We knew he was here this afternoon, so what happened between you two?"

"You *knew?*"

"Don't bother to feign being shocked, Josie. Why won't you just admit you like the man? He has done nothing against you and has indeed tried to give you anything you need. Why will you not accept his assistance? He cares for you."

"Sally—I appreciate that you are newly happy and that you want things to be easy for me. This is not the first time I have had such a conversation. You have seen the men from the Dove that have tried to 'rescue' me . . ."

"This is different," she protested. "None of them have done so much good. And I see the way you look at—"

"That is enough."

"No, it isn't. Not nearly." Sally sat down on the edge of the bed. "I am not under your financial support anymore and I do consider you a friend, so I hope that I may speak freely. You insist on making things difficult for yourself, even when an opportunity to make things better practically lands in your lap."

That called up an image that Josephine would rather not dwell on. She sat up straighter and tied her robe in irritation.

"I appreciate your candor, but you forget that it is not just my fate in balance here, but the majority of the girls at the Dove."

"So, tell him that," she said simply.

"You are mad."

"I know it sounds shocking, Josie, but you could try to trust someone."

"That is another luxury that I cannot afford," she exhaled.

"Why not?" Sally insisted, anger rising in her voice. "What Mother is doing—kidnapping and selling girls—would be punishable if you could prove it. Being associated with a man of Lennox's stature and reputation . . ."

"Sally, my darling. It is far too dangerous for everyone involved."

"Fine then," she returned, shoving her bonnet back on her head. "Sit here miserable, save a few girls a year, scribble your high-and-mighty ideas. When it comes to putting them into action, this time with help, you balk."

Josephine sat up as far as she could, but she was definitely not in a position of authority, in a too-small silk robe, adrift in the blankets which still radiated with the duke's body temperature.

"Lennox does not wish to be a crusader. By all accounts, even your precious Nicholas would tell you this, Elias must abide by the stringent rules of his dukedom. He would never be a disappointment or shame to his family name. I am the worst sort of woman for him."

Sally shook her head sadly.

"You don't even know, Josie. You never asked him."

There was silence between them until Sally, newly confident, bowed her head regally.

"I have a carriage waiting. You know where to find me, should you need me."

CHAPTER SEVEN

"I want to believe that there are those who will not be able to easily dismiss my words, but I do not have much hope. I know that society is comfortable with a certain way of doing things and dislikes complication. Dear Readers, do not think me an unrepentant cynic. I am simply aware of our shared reality. Though I will not hesitate to speak out against the order of things, I do not believe that it will do much to change them."
—FROM *ON SOCIETY'S ILLS AND THE REAL PRICE OF PROSTITUTION* BY JOSEPHINE GRANT

Elias told Dryden that he wanted to be left alone and to make up any excuse that he saw fit. He stared at a wall for a long while. He drank a few glasses of brandy. He lit a fire when the sun went down, and he dressed for bed. When he took off his coat, a scrap of paper fell out of the pocket. It was the slip that he had been using as a bookmark. He had not given it much notice at the shop, but he now saw that it read "Doesn't Matter" in Josephine's tight cursive. He recognized her handwriting from the impressive notes in the margins of the Peacock book and from her waspish inscription to him in her own book.

Doesn't matter: The sentiment was greatly galling, if it referred to him at all. She could have been talking about the price of tea, for all he knew.

It was just another mystery, he told himself. Just another peculiar piece of her riddle, which he doubted anyone would solve. He wrote to Uncle Harrington to tell him the matter had been resolved and that no further investigation was necessary. He mulled over whether or not to also call off the reconnaissance on Josephine herself, and decided to let that wait for now. It could not hurt to know her whereabouts, even if he intended to stay in his house.

He had sent Thackeray back home, told him to enjoy what he had with Sally. Elias told him to make it known that he would not be entertaining visitors for at least a fortnight. Alessandra tried to call early the next day, but he warned her against contracting the illness he had; she would not want her face to puff up so. That was effective in keeping her away. He had Dryden inform the duchess of his fabricated sickness. The footman was so kind as to add that the doctor had already seen him and it was a simple, but emphatically contagious head cold.

Elias stepped back from the Josephine Grant Situation. Completely.

He did not shave for a few days, a luxury, read some mythology, not at all helpful, wrote various correspondences, and lined up Josephine's cursed books on the enormous shelf next to his bed. His chambers were of the greatest advantage in the house, and he enjoyed three days of the sun setting and rising in a reassuring manner. He started to come to his senses.

He determined he would let the investigation of Josephine continue until the end of the week and then cancel the contract. It would ease his mind to know that she had reverted to her normal routine, and he would go back to his. It was clearly what she wanted, after all. She had implied, using the absurd qualifier of "Byronic" scandal, that association with her would bring shame on his family and draw the ire of society.

She had more or less said that there was no earthly chance they could be together, after throwing herself at him and before falling cozily asleep against his thumping heart. He had lain awake for a while after she had drifted off, learning that she snored and muttered in her sleep, but when Dryden came to fetch him, the picture they made together faded. For the hour that they were unconscious, they had gotten along fine. Awake, and talking, they were a lost cause.

When he had kissed the mussed tresses of her head, wispy from the steam of the bath, he determined it would be the last time he would touch her. He was not a man who made final decisions lightly. What he went through the next week, while pretending to be sick, was like a mourning period. Done and done.

Thus, when Friday came to his door, he was still hesitant to let the world back in. There was a letter, already sealed, sitting on the desk in his study that officially called off the surveillance of Miss Josephine Grant of the Paper Garden. He had signed it, wax sealed it, and addressed it himself. It had been sitting there for three days.

That morning, he lay in bed awaiting his valet's knock and scratching his beard. He would miss it, especially now that the chill in the air was reaching a high note. He wondered if Josephine would like it. Surely, she would complain at least about the scrape of it against the sensitive skin of her cheek. He would never know for sure, but he thought she might also find it fetching. He needed to stop wondering all these things about her, her opinion of anything he thought of, what she would want to have for breakfast. It was Friday and it was time to get ready for the rigors of the dinners and dances and politics. If he possessed any more ready excuses to shield against reality, he needed them now. He kept his eyes closed, awaiting a brilliant idea.

None came.

So he yawned and stretched and pulled his body from the sheets wound around him in his fidgety sleep. He braced himself on the edge of the bed, hands splayed. What did he have to do today? His schedule sat open to the correct day on his nightstand, but he did not need to look: luncheon with the Francis family and various others, dinner with the same group at Lord Frost's, before the ball that would occur in Frost's expansive residence. His cousin Sebastian had just returned from extensive foreign travel, and it was something of a welcome home. His mother had sent various notes during the week with a reminder of the very important day and that she did hope he would be well enough to fulfill his duties. It was thinly veiled, but when mother mentioned "duty," it meant "you will absolutely obey my edict to do whatever time-wasting social activity I have planned."

His door burst open.

In it stood Nicholas, panting, and Alessandra behind him, at his left shoulder. She was clutching and unclutching her hands.

"Pardon the intrusion," Alessandra started.

"You must come with us," Nicholas finished.

Elias shrugged on a dressing gown, unperturbed.

"I am just waking. I have not even begun my morning ritual." He yawned yet again and attempted to sit down at his shaving kit. Nicholas, per usual, just kept on talking.

"Elias. Miss Francis's father is on his way here to secure your declaration of betrothal. That is what your mother and he plan to do today—throw you two together this afternoon, allow time for a proposal from you, make the announcement at the ball."

Elias looked to his sister.

"It is not a joke," she said. "Mother told me over breakfast. I sent for Nicholas. Mama is sure you are ready to declare."

"Without even a by-your-leave," he said, stunned. He was staring at his hands, sturdy blue veins pumping at the top indicating that his heart was still working, though he suspected that was not the case. He did not think the time would come so soon. His voice was dull, but even, and resigned. "But why should she ask me? Everyone has decided that I shall marry the huge-eyed heiress. I have given no evidence to the contrary. I suppose there would really be no reason to ask me . . . my entire existence is implied."

"We do not have time to discuss it," Alessandra said, donning a smart bonnet. Elias noticed then that she was already in her pelisse and ready to travel. "Mother is changing and giving orders for luncheon. Nicholas's carriage is in the back. You must get in it now."

Dryden had entered while she was talking and gathered the necessary components of his master's daily wear. Elias blinked and rubbed his eyes. Was there a remote chance he was still sleeping?

"No." He looked at Nicholas, then Alessandra again. "No, no."

"Right," Nicholas agreed. "No. No, you will not be here to fulfill their plans. We are going to Sally's new flat, just outside of London, no one will intrude there. Lennox—move."

They heard an echoing knock on the front door and a butler scurrying to answer it. Nicholas and Alessandra were right: there was no time. It unfroze his limbs and he yanked on his overcoat, right over his dressing gown, and mashed a hat onto his head. He would worry about his appearance when he was in a safe place, which Ashworth Hall was not, for the first time in his life.

"Thank you," he said to his two best friends, his sister and the man who might as well be his brother. "Thank you."

"Shhh, Eli, Mama will hear you."

Alessandra marched down the hallway, but Nicholas fell into step beside him and Dryden trailed behind the pair with an armful of clothes.

"They will not shackle you today," Nicholas smiled. "Not today."

◆　◆　◆

Josephine knew that she had to apologize to Sally for being so irrational, but she felt entirely silly waiting in the entryway with an armful of flowers like a chastised gentleman caller. Sally's new domicile was a good balance of livable and opulent, with more than a few flounces designed to flaunt Nicholas's wealth and devotion to his mistress. Golden cherubs danced around the mirror next to her, a mirror that also revealed Josephine's own less-than-ideal state, wisps of brown hair flying above the line of her scalp, trying to escape the fire in her brain underneath. She had been alone for days, except for Sapphire, who had volunteered to take Sally's place at the Paper Garden.

Sally's maid—*her maid!*—had gone to tell her mistress—*her mistress!*—of the arrival of Miss Grant. Josephine stood awkwardly in the hallway, shifting from foot to foot, grazing a hand over all the surfaces. She couldn't believe that it was only a week ago that the young girl had been living in her home, like a sister. Josephine looked up as a door closed. Lost in thought, she assumed it was the maid returning.

Instead, it was Elias, sheet white, but looking at her like she was the ghost.

Neither of them said a word. He was dressed in a hasty manner—messy cravat, waistcoat unbuttoned—almost as if he just gotten out of bed and threw on clothing with a bleary eye. His hair bolted up in competing factions on his head, unable to come to a consensus about which side to choose. His face was partially obscured by what had to be a week's worth of beard growth and his eyes had sunken further, pooled and cradled by tired skin.

When they both chose to speak, they did so at the same time.

"What are you doing here?"

"Do not get any irrational ideas," he ran on. "I've only just gotten here and I may as well have been kidnapped. What are *you* doing here?"

"Visiting my friend; this is perfectly within my rights. I could not have known you would be here." The stems of the bouquet made a crunching sound under the anxious tightening of her fist.

A smile cracked the hard lines on his face. "Then why have you brought me flowers?"

The maid cleared her throat.

"Pardon? Miss Grant? The lady says she is occupied . . ."

Her eyes darted toward the duke.

". . . but that she would welcome an evening visit, should you be able to come back."

Elias turned to the maid.

"It is all right, Mildred. They are trying to protect me. As it seems I have already been revealed to Miss Grant, we will retire together to the sitting room. Tea would be appreciated. Also, could you be a dear and put my flowers in a vase?"

The woman nodded, taking the bouquet from Josephine, and went on her way.

"Why so many lilies? I hate lilies." Elias put a hand on the small of her back and directed her toward the sitting room.

"Sally loves lilies and I am an ass," Josephine said.

"What did you do now?"

"It is nothing of your concern," she replied, stopping outside the door. "Perhaps I should just go, return as Sally requested."

"Nonsense," he said, shuttling her into the room. "Sally will be delighted. We are all discussing my future, you will find it entertaining."

The scene within was strangely familial, Sally and Nicholas sitting together on a settee and Alessandra picking at a decimated plate of scones. The curtains were drawn over the windows and the lack of natural light created a kind of suspended world, blotted out the afternoon.

"Josie," Sally exclaimed, rising immediately. "I'm sorry, I did not expect you today and we—the duke—has a bit of an emergency."

Josephine noticed the duke's eyes roamed too freely, not settling on any one thing, and there was a glaze to the pinpointed pupils. Panic bubbled in her throat. He was sick. That had to be it. She squeezed the arm she still held and he tried to focus on her, but failed. How had she not seen it? Pale, bedraggled—every terrible disease and affliction sprung to the forefront of her mind on a wave of horror.

"Emergency?" she croaked.

"No emergency. I am fine," he said, even though it was clear to her that he was not fine, not at all.

"Miss Grant," Alessandra said, joining them in a tight little circle. Elias broke off and stumbled to a corner near Nicholas and assumed a cockeyed leaning position. Josephine's eyes followed him with worry. "It is quite serendipitous that you are here. None of us have been successful talking sense into Elias; you may be our only hope."

"I assure you that I have had no luck in that area."

Josephine had meant it as a lighthearted jab, but Elias's face was turned to the wall and did not display any amusement. She was not sure he had heard.

"Do tell me what is happening," Josephine said to Alessandra. Sally opened the door quietly to let in Mildred and the tea. That was accomplished in total silence, and then she looked directly at him again. "Lennox—please. Are you sick?"

"Darling—no—but did someone give me laudanum?" He wobbled and then elbowed Nicholas. "Nicholas."

"You needed it," Nicholas replied with a shrug.

"I am not sick." His eyebrows drew together. "I have been drugged."

"You were hysterical," Nicholas said.

Sally laughed and Alessandra frowned.

"I do apologize, Miss Grant," said the young Lady Addison. "It is uncommonly rude for them to go on as such without telling you of the situation that brought us here. Lennox is not ill; he is simply insisting on being too noble."

"Then this is not an emergency. He is always too noble." Josephine smiled. She could not help but find it funny, seeing the duke unable to comport himself in an upright manner. He was staring at the shadow of his hand on the wall.

Nicholas reached for the tea. "Funny, Miss Grant, but it is not so straightforward. Lennox has been trying to tell us that he is willing to marry a woman he does not love in order to secure his financial estate and make certain Alessandra's reputation is snowy white."

"I would rather he be happy," Alessandra said softly. "He should not marry Miss Francis, no matter Mama's wishes."

"We ran this afternoon," Elias said, "but you are both wrong in thinking we can outrun the duchess."

Josephine had little idea what they were talking about and no context in which to answer. Sally saw the quizzical look on her face and took pity on her.

"Lennox's mother wants him to marry the second daughter of an earl, one Miss Francis," she explained. "This morning, her father came to Ashworth Hall unannounced, but Alessandra knew that the duchess had invited Lord Francis to talk to Elias about a happy union between the two. I believe Alessandra and Nic pulled the duke out of his house before he could entirely collect his thoughts, much less his clothing."

"I am woozy," Elias said, "but I know that we have made a fatal mistake. Mother is probably raging around the hearth, and it will be ten times worse that I was not there to be ambushed."

Everyone, except him, was looking at Josephine.

"He is right," she confirmed. "He must marry her."

That pronouncement brought his eyes to her, sad and grateful. The motion of his head threw off his equilibrium again and his hand tried to find purchase on the wall, but slid. Josephine fought the urge to go to him, to hold up his unsteady, adorable frame and tell him that she . . .

Thankfully, he spoke before she could finish the thought in her mind.

"She makes more sense than the lot of you combined," he said, nodding to them. "I feel seasick. Are we moving?"

"Josie," Sally entreated, "you cannot be serious about the duke marrying Miss Francis."

"I am quite serious," she said, folding her hands tightly to stop the shaking. "Forgive me, but Lennox is not getting any younger. If this heiress can provide a proper dowry and a suitable reputation to ease Alessandra's introduction to society, then she is perfect. Your family will not allow the opportunity to pass. I assume that she is of childbearing age, Elias?"

He nodded mutely. No one in the room acknowledged the slip of his first name in mixed company—there was no longer a need to pretend that the assembled group did not know exactly what was going on.

"Then . . . she is perfect."

"Madness," Alessandra interjected, drawing up a regal bearing that was very convincing for a girl of fifteen. "I read your book. You hate that the world works this way."

"Yes, but that does not mean I can change it. If Miss Francis is amiable, the duke has no excuse."

"Miss Grant, you care for him." Alessandra's eyes glittered like her brother's when she was incensed. "He cares for you."

"Allie," Elias warned from the corner.

Nicholas drained the rest of his tea and set the cup down with an authoritative click.

"You two are the most insensible sensible people I have ever known," he said, getting up from the settee to scoop Sally into his arms. "Come, ladies, let us find less tedious activities while Miss Grant helps the duke right his wardrobe. He still looks a mess, does he not?"

The ladies giggled, nearly muffling Josephine's reply.

"Oh, no, I must be—"

She felt her protest cut short by the electric touch of Elias's fingertips on her forearm.

"Stay," he said, only loud enough for her to hear. "Even if just a few minutes. I cannot go without telling you a few things if this is truly good-bye."

❖ ❖ ❖

When the gaggle of conspirators had left the sitting room, Elias pulled Josephine into his arms. He was still rickety and her face swam, but it was not unpleasant to give way to the drug running through his system. She was standing before him and he could enjoy that. He had mourned the past week, yes, and one of his prevailing thoughts had been that he had not said a proper good-bye. He had not told her the thing that he burned to tell her now, even if it seemed irrational and unwise. She was trembling, so he tightened his grip and just held her.

"I appreciate that you got them to listen to reason," he said into her neck, the neck which he wished he could burrow in and hide, for a few lifetimes. "I appreciate it more than you can ever know. You are the one above reproach."

"I cannot believe you brought your sister to a house of ill repute."

"I did not," he said, pulling back to look at her, appalled. "*They* practically threw me into Nicholas's carriage. With the news of the arrival of Lord Francis and the fact that I had just awoken, I could not think straight. All I could think—"

"Yes?"

"I only thought: I do not want to marry the girl."

"She may not want to marry you, either," she said with a light flick to his nose.

"Virago," he scolded. "Even if she does want to marry me, she will regret it."

Because there will always be another in my heart, his mind filled in as he ran a thumb along her soft bottom lip. He pushed down the urge to kiss her, knowing it would make the conversation all the more difficult. They stood entwined, but they may as well have been a million miles apart.

"That is not true. You will be a dutiful husband."

"Of course I will." He held her cheek, gazing down at the face he saw constantly in his fantasies. "I must. But know this—I do not love her. I think I am in love with y—"

She squirmed away, pointing a finger in warning.

"No. If *that* is what you needed to tell me, Elias, I plead that you keep it to yourself. It is the laudanum speaking."

"Doesn't matter, eh?" He savored the moment that she realized he had read and interpreted her little notes to herself, all around the Paper Garden. It ate up the air between them and she flushed. "Changes nothing?"

"Both are true and you know it as surely as I."

"I do not," he said, with more heat than he expected, grasping her forearms. "I do not know enough about you to know if I could change anything, if it matters. You will not trust me enough to do so, though I have done everything short of bring you the heavens. Now I must marry and the pretense of you being my mistress will not hold. Your lack of faith in me has made the situation impossible. I have thought it all over in circles. Even if your family had been involved in a most terrible scandal, you were indeed raised a lady, and we could have found a way. It cannot be just that. There is something else."

He searched her face for a clue, but her lips descended on his before he could read her expression. He responded in kind to her kiss but pulled back much sooner than he wanted. The damn woman was always trying to control things.

"Unjust," he lectured. "If you want to be equal with men, you need to stop wielding your feminine wiles so effectively."

"That was your good-bye kiss."

"Well then it was rubbish and we will have to do it again."

"This," she reflected, skittering her fingertips across his beard, just as he imagined she would, "is curious. It makes a pricklier embrace, but you do look dashing and dangerous."

"Oh? I thought you might like it."

"Do shave before you propose to Miss Francis."

"Perhaps she will say no if I do not?" he asked hopefully.

"Perhaps. You look like an unrepentant rogue."

"Do I now?" He raised an eyebrow. "An unrepentant rogue alone with a beautiful woman. I suppose I have no choice but to ravish you, as is my nature."

She put a hand to his mouth to stop his swooping.

"You think I do not trust you, but that is not the right of it. I do trust you. I think you noble and loyal. I respect you. This is part of the reason why I cannot tell you everything. You gave up Oxford to fulfill the obligations of your station in life and quite honestly, my family history and current employment would negate that sacrifice. It would come with a mess of new problems that I have created myself."

She kissed his temple and the hair that feathered there, barely a touch.

"I do trust you and I want to keep your counsel. I even want to tell you mundane things such as how annoying the birds outside of my window were this morning. I have more faith in you than any man I have ever known. I simply do not want to ruin your life."

"Josie-not-Josie, woman," he said, feeling the seasickness turning into something crashed on a shore. It loosened his tongue, gave it a beseeching tone, but he didn't care. He would blame it all on the altered state later, but he would very well tell her his true feelings now. "Whoever you are, whatever you have done . . . by god, I cannot imagine never seeing you again."

"Eli, please," she said, with a new ache in her voice. She nestled her face against his and he felt her pointy little nose in his beard. "Your sister is right. I care for you. I also know to my very core that the only place I can occupy in your life is mistress. I could not do that. I will not do that. It would . . ."

Josephine didn't finish her sentence right away, so he finished it for her.

"It would never be enough."

This led to a vast and yawning silence.

"I do not want you as a mistress," he said, soft enough to honor the quiet. "I thought that was clear. I want you, but I do not want that."

"And that leaves us?"

"Back where we started."

"Your clothes!" she exclaimed, as if it just occurred to her why they had been standing there, in each other's arms. "Nicholas was correct, though it was a see-through ruse to get us alone. You are still a mess."

He looked down at himself: cravat askew and barely tied or folded, pants not quite tucked into his boots, and dear god—his waistcoat was buttoned askew. Josephine noticed the same thing and snickered.

"Come on then," she grinned, pulling the cravat by one end until it completely unwound. "We shall make you presentable."

They both realized how provocative the action was when it was already too late. It made time stand still, stopped both of them from talking incessantly. Or at all. Neither of them ruined the moment with words, but in one unbroken motion he had swept her onto the settee. The linen cloth fell to the floor beside it in a coil.

Her fingers fumbled blindly at his waistcoat buttons.

"Better get this off, too," she said into his kiss.

"Necessary, yes, good."

She ran her hands across his chest, pulling the coat back. He moved his shoulders as helpfully as he could, as long as it did not inhibit his main goal at the moment, pinning her beneath him and stealing the exhales from her mouth. The remains of the laudanum still thrummed in his veins, making it easier to forget his conduct. He let his fingertips wander where only his eyes had before and grazed a thumb over her nipple before he even knew what he was doing. It was as if they had wandered into one of his half-formed dreams, all glowing and unreal. The lazy circle he made earned him a low moan, a sound that cracked every bit of gentlemanly reserve he had been saving. His hands went everywhere, wanted to be everywhere on her body all at once.

"The door is not locked," she said against his cheek, though she did not cease her own explorations of his torso.

"They will not be back so soon. They think you will convince me of my mistake." He kept kissing her as he spoke, elongating the two sentences. His hands had stolen their way under her skirts and onto sturdy stockings unlike the ones she wore at the Dove. He flashed a wicked smile, teasing her released an outrageous feeling of happiness in him. "You are not wearing stays, how shameful."

As he had hoped, she scowled close to his face. He could feel the expression against his skin.

"I am not going to a ball, this is a day dress and besides, I had not thought to be here more than a few minutes."

"You must tire of being wrong," he said, biting her earlobe. He ran a hand along the length of her leg, long and shapely. She trembled. If he had to go to Lord Frost's ball tonight and end up engaged to be married, he would take all that Josephine would allow him now, for it would be the last time he could do it without disrespecting the both of them. If he could not take his pleasure, he wanted to at least give her something to remember him by. With a silent entreaty to any listening god that she would not slap him, he stole a hand under the rough fabric of her chemise.

❖   ❖   ❖

She lost all of her breath in one whoosh when Elias's fingers found the most sensitive spot on her body. She was shocked, coursed to the bone with pleasure, but shocked that he would be so bold. Neither of them was in possession of their wits at the current moment, yet still—his sense of propriety had gone out of the window posthaste when faced with their imminent separation. Once he had pushed her chemise up, she was overwhelmed with wanting him—all of him. It was a sensation she did not feel often, being that her nights were spent surrounded by disgusting, licentious men who activated no lust in her. She had tried to rationalize her attraction to Elias, but as his fingers found their target, she finally knew for certain that there was no rationale.

He could ruin her, for all she cared.

She clung to his neck, feeling like she might faint, or no—just dizzy? Yes, dizzy, that was it. The room was spinning because her eyes were shut so tight. She thought her face must be bright red. She whimpered, feeling his finger move back and forth slowly on the core of her heat, made all the smoother by the sudden rush of slickness that had come with her excitement. These things that she had imagined him doing in her secret thoughts . . . he was doing all that and on a steady path toward more, his right hand between her legs firmly, working some sort of magic. It was nothing in comparison to the fumbling experimentation of her youth.

"Tell me to stop, love," he said thickly.

"No, I mean, yes," she managed. "Don't. I can't."

Even though she could not speak in complete sentences, Elias understood her. He gave her another slow kiss as he stroked under her skirts, his lips in languid duet with his clever hands. He was half on top of her, half perched precariously on the settee, all single-minded. All she could do was weave her hands through his hair and attempt to kiss him back, but she kept getting distracted by what his fingers were doing.

All pretense of trying to keep up with him became moot when he slipped one long digit inside of her. She moaned and her head lolled back. For the fleeting moment that her eyes flew open, she saw a rakish grin on his face.

"Unrepentant rogue," he said in a voice darker than she had ever heard from him.

She squirmed.

"No one asked you to repent," she exhaled, bucking slightly as his thumb caressed the soft, ecstatic center of her. Her barbed remark, so difficult to form, was lost in a murmur of sounds that she did not think were words. Her eyes fluttered shut again. She could not look at him; the sensation was so intense. He moved another digit inside her and she pushed her pelvis toward him, flooded with a swift and aching need.

"That look on your face," he whispered. "Oh god."

He pressed the hard length of himself against her in a desperate, involuntary way and cupped her breast. His desire for her increased the blinding white light that had been building behind her eyelids. She felt a distinct wish to hear her real name in his lust-colored tenor, so instead she just moaned his own over and over as her consciousness exploded. She shuddered into him, feeling the most connected to another person she had ever experienced and also curiously outside of herself. Detached from the walls that she had built around her heart.

After she had calmed, he withdrew his hand from the layers of her skirts carefully. She crawled back into his arms and he hugged her tight, anchoring her against his slim and tight torso. She didn't have any words.

"I thought you could not be more beautiful, but in the throes of ecstasy . . . you are a goddess," he said with sincere reverence. "To think that is the only time I will see—"

"Shhh, darling. None of that."

She put an arm around his lithe frame and buried her face. Strangely, she felt as if she might weep. She was not the hysterical kind.

It also was not as if this was the first time a man had given her pleasure, but—it was distinctly different. Emotional. Horrifying, unwanted feelings surged to the forefront of her mind, unhinged by the climax.

She came crashing back into reality. What in the world had they done? Lost all control, and on Sally's settee, at that. An unlocked door that could have been opened at any moment. She sat up and pulled at her wrinkled clothing. She felt a rush of embarrassment—what a wanton she was, allowing this to happen. The man was capable of making her lose herself completely.

"Oh no," Elias said. "I see what is happening. You are already analyzing again. I know many ways we can stop that process. Shall I take you back to the Paper Garden? We can steal an afternoon. Josie, it is possible."

"That is not my name," she said, terse with defensiveness.

"Do not snap at me," he returned. "Not now."

Josephine resolved to blame it all on the blasted laudanum and his lowered inhibitions, yet she still could not believe she had let her passion master her so.

"This is uncomfortable. We must get you dressed."

He fixed her with his odd amber eyes commandingly.

"Very well. But you will not shut down on me. I will dress and we will talk—with not a wink involved and no lies. Judging by Alessandra's whims, she will grow bored in ten more minutes. Talk to me without defending yourself with sarcasm for those ten minutes. You owe me that, at the least."

She picked up his waistcoat.

"Always making bargains," she muttered. "You really would do smashingly in the House of Lords."

"I said no sarcasm."

◆   ◆   ◆

Elias bent down to retrieve his cravat, his pants still painfully tight. He had expected her idyllic state to carry them back to her house. Since that did not seem to be the case, he had to grasp to prolong their time together.

"I was not being sarcastic. You would do fine in Lords, but better back at Oxford, which is where you will end up."

He walked to a mirror standing in the corner, snapping the creased cloth. He slung it around his neck and began tying it into a Mail Coach, the easiest knot he knew, though it still could look sharp. Josephine was smiling behind him, holding out his topcoat.

"Your Grace," she prodded. He shrugged into the coat, enjoying the intimacy of it, as if she had come into his bedroom in the middle of his morning ritual. "You know, I assumed that you did not tie your own cravats, that such artistry could not be the work of a coddled duke."

"Brummell tied his."

Josephine rolled her eyes at the mention of the notorious dandy, who bore little resemblance to Elias in any manner, except perhaps that they both had excellent tailors.

"You are no dandy," she said.

"I am impeccable, though," he smiled fondly at her reflection. "Am I not?"

"Not at the moment," she chided, flattening his hair though she had to stand on her tiptoes to do it.

Elias figured he should not delay telling her his feelings.

"I thought I was ready to be virtuous and dependable, but I am not." He flipped one side of the tie in a skillful tug. "I cannot let you go."

"Elias," she sighed, so close that he felt it on the back of his neck. It did not help his unfulfilled desire for her. "You are expected to declare to Miss Francis. When you get home, your mother will be livid. She will browbeat you into proposing, am I wrong? Your silence answers that. We both must do the right thing and that means going in different directions."

"That has little to do with your pigheadedness. It is an excuse." He finished the ends of the cravat and faced her. She began to button his coat without prompting and once again, the normally innocuous gesture was sexually charged. Her fingers on the cold metal of the buttons were too suggestive. He cleared his throat.

"What I am saying, Miss-Whomever-You-Are, is that you mustn't forget that it is *you* who has not given *me* a chance. You refuse me information, using a vague scandal as a shield, though for all you know, my mother might adore you. I think that she would. You are both so stubborn and unruly."

"Silliness, Eli. Your mother would not tolerate the presence of such a commoner."

"Another assumption." He smoothed his pants, tucking the bottom hems into his boots much neater than before. His head was beginning to clear, both from the medicine and the vehemence of his longing. "Tell me something truly. Why did you flee to Scotland with your mother? If your father was titled, as you say, he would have supported you monetarily no matter what. You could have enjoyed safety and security at the very least. Why get in the middle of a fight that is not yours?"

"My father was not a good man," she stated baldly.

"Gambling? Drinking? Hell-raking?"

"All of the above."

"Ah." He studied her in the mirror. "Why come back to England, then?"

"I acquired the Paper Garden when he died. I told you."

"Oh, did you? No—Josephine Grant did, and that is not your name, as you just barked at me."

"Josephine Grant is the name on the lease, but I assure you it was my father's shop. I am surprised that you did not find a history of transfers of the deed."

"Curiously, the records office could not find them. It is as if they disappeared."

"Curious indeed," she said saucily, looking for a moment as if she was enjoying the questioning.

"Was the lease ever even in your real name?"

"Like a foxhound, you are," she said with a sideways smile, unable to keep a proper amount of distance between them. They were again wrapped around each other, but now fully clothed. He was about as proper as he was going to get without access to his accoutrements back at Ashworth.

"Not that it will help you in finding my real name," she continued, "but in the interest of your request for truth, the lease was under the name of my father's mistress, which is how it could possibly come into my hands in the first place. It was the only piece of unentailed land, all the rest went to a male cousin."

"A cousin still in Staffordshire?"

"I have no way of knowing that."

He raised an eyebrow, doubting.

"It is the truth, if vague," she said.

"Stay with me until they make me marry her," he blurted, surprising himself. "We can drag the engagement out, see what happens."

"Elias . . ." Her voice was melancholy now. "It is against my entire philosophy and besides, I cannot allow you to continue frequenting the Sleeping Dove. It is no place for an upright duke who is a rare credit to the nobility."

"Thackeray brought me to the Dove to cheer me up, you know. He thought me dour."

"I think you dour."

There were the matching footsteps in the hallway, same as at the Paper Garden: Alessandra, light and quick, Sally, wide and bright, Nicholas, loud and convincing. Elias released Josephine with great reluctance as the door opened.

"Well, now, my divine ladies," Nicholas said, florid as always. "The duke looks as if he has achieved a modicum of respectability. We should face the music back at Ashworth, eh? Someone—Alessandra, you—should come up with a plausible story."

Sally was making a gesture at Josephine, sort of waving her hand around her face, at once frantic while trying to be discreet. Elias turned to Josephine and realized that her entire soft, smooth face looked as if it had been dragged repeatedly across the carpet. He had to stifle a laugh when she looked back at him with those wide blue eyes, questioning. He simply stroked his beard suggestively.

"Rogue," she hissed askance.

"Unrepentant," he sang. "See me. Tomorrow. The Dove."

"Relentless."

"Do you want us to leave?" Nicholas asked impishly.

"No, Thackeray," Elias said a notch louder. "We must return home. Miss Grant has honored my request to continue our conversation about my fate tomorrow and we have already wasted enough time while Mother is at home waiting."

"I have a genius idea for an excuse," Alessandra said, full of intrigue and animation. And, apparently, romantic notions . . . she looked hopefully to Josephine. "So, he will not marry Miss Francis? He *cannot*, look at you two."

Josephine and Elias glanced down at their hands, still entwined. Josephine dropped the clutch and cleared her throat.

"He must, Lady Addison, but it will be all right."

"He will not. He will not marry her." She flounced her skirts into a curtsey. "Good day, ladies, I do thank you for the sanctuary, hospitality, and pleasure of your company."

Elias thought his sister's maturity downright disturbing at times. She wore a triumphant, knowing smile when she turned toward the door.

Elias caught Josephine's chin and held it. "Tomorrow?"

"Fine," she sighed.

Even her resignation was a triumph. He smiled and followed the rest of his party.

◆   ◆   ◆

Sally sat down at the tea table and beckoned Josephine to join her.

"Josephine," she said carefully, pouring tea for both of them. "You need to tell me why you're acting like a madwoman."

She accepted the tea gratefully and sighed, lounging into the chair. She had to admit it to herself, perhaps to Sally. She was mad for the man. What had just transpired between them proved it beyond a shadow of a doubt.

"He has turned my life upside down."

Sally smiled.

"I know the feeling." She took her friend's hand and patted it. "But, darling, you are driving all of us crazy. It is apparent to anyone who sees you with him that you don't simply admire him. Admit it or not, it does not change the fact that you want to be with that man."

"I am sorry that we argued. I want to admit fault. I cannot . . . he is making it impossible to think straight."

"I saw the flowers, thank you. And of course I forgive you." Sally sipped her tea, peering at Josephine with keen eyes over the lip of the cup. "He is not thinking straight himself. You should have seen him when he arrived. Still in his sleeping shirt, wild-eyed, frightened—and not at the prospect of marriage, at the prospect of losing you."

"You should not have given him laudanum."

"I didn't give it to him, Nicholas did." Sally's lip curled slyly. "He raved something fierce for a half an hour afterward. Your Elias mutters under his breath more than he talks to other people, normally, but he didn't seem shy about telling us that he adores you. He said, 'I don't care if she bathes in virgin blood or turns into a wolf at the full moon, there is not another woman I will marry.'"

"He said that?" Josephine blinked.

"And more, but it got quite tedious. Nicholas threw a pillow at him and we all had a laugh. He calmed down shortly before you got here." Sally was doing an awful amount of smirking, Josephine thought. "Of course, from the looks of your neck, perhaps he didn't exactly calm down. He mauled you."

"Sally!"

"Well."

"Oh, gods," Josephine said into her hands.

"The beard does give him a tempting, brooding look," she continued, watching her reaction sideways.

"Stop, stop." Josephine peeked through her fingers. "I take your point."

"You know that he is a good man," Sally said, her tone turning serious. "I know you thought that good men did not exist, but you cannot continue treating him like he is a myth. He will help you. Tell him everything!"

"I have not even told *you* everything!"

"Oh, I know," Sally waved a hand. "Woman of mystery. Josie is not your name, etc., etc."

"He told all of you?"

"I said he was babbling, dear heart."

"I do . . . care for Lennox." It was still difficult to force the words out of her mouth, but perhaps saying them aloud would help ease the heartache. A little pit opened in her stomach. "And I believe he feels the same for me. However . . ."

"Oh, here we are with the 'however' . . ."

"However, there is no telling if he would shoulder the burden of the truth about the Dove, or if it would change the way he felt about me."

"Well. You cannot know that if you do not tell him." Sally set her tea cup down, leaving the dregs in the bottom. She had never done that while still living at the Garden, as the tea had been too scarce to waste.

"I do not . . ."

" . . . want to risk it? You would rather watch him enter into a love-less marriage and likely a life of regrets? For both of you? How noble." She snorted in disapproval.

"He would not be in danger, then, and I—well, I am used to it."

"Or you tell him and he helps and we all escape it together."

"Sally." She threw her napkin on the table. "What, happily ever after?"

"Yes."

"Unlikely."

Sally sighed a long-suffering sigh.

"All right then, my friend. I tried."

"Do you really think he would not cast me aside?"

"Darling, I think he would do everything in his power to stop the injustices. I think he would be enraged." She paused, looking away. "I am not going back to the Dove. Neither should you. Find another way to keep the shop open."

"But the girls . . ."

"You can't save all of them. You can't even save yourself, as it stands. Mother is increasingly suspicious of you. What if she learns you've been sheltering girls? If she finds out, she will bar you from the club—or worse."

The bluntness of the statement seemed to hit Josephine in the chest.

"You mean she will kill me." Josephine let out a long breath. "I ought to speak with Elias."

Sally just nodded.

"Good. More tea?"

CHAPTER EIGHT

"It is, of course, much easier for a literary character to take a risk for love. The realities of social strata and responsibility mean nothing but a plot point in today's modern literature, but outside of these stories we are not pushing for change. The ideals we embody in our art rarely play themselves out in our lives. What would happen if we took the example of our fictional heroes; what if each of us was a Don Juan?"
—From *The Collected Essays of Lord Elias Addison*

Elias managed to avoid his mother's ire by way of a little white lie—"I most certainly told you that I would be away from Ashworth this afternoon; I had a meeting with the solicitor regarding one of the country estates." He had blinked like an innocent at her wrath, insisting that he could not be expected to know that Lord Francis would be visiting when he had not been informed. That much was the truth.

Still, Sophia stared daggers at him all through the meal. Lord Sebastian Frost, his cousin and heir of the Earl of Harrington, prattled on about the lovely time he spent in India and how good it was to be back in "civilization." He knew Sebastian was lying through his teeth. Elias had received letters to the contrary: *"Cousin, it is stiflingly hot here. In stark contrast are the women, who are lukewarm at best. They seem immune to my charms and are too smart by half. Could you send me a decent brandy, by the by?"*, but as long as he dominated the conversation, Elias only had to smile and nod at Miss Francis on occasion, who sat obediently at his shoulder. For her part, she looked as if she was paying even less attention than he was.

By the time guests began arriving for the ball, Elias, Nicholas, and Sebastian had installed themselves in a corner, hoping to fend off the marriage market by presenting a united trio of backs.

Frost's grand ballroom was beyond magnificent—it was decadent to the point of embarrassing. His parties, which had been sorely missed while he was abroad, were ever in demand. Even though the patronesses thought him an unmarriageable rake, invitations to his events were sought after for matchmaking and gossip. Elias had seen a woman vomit in a potted plant at one of these ordeals and then go on her merry way with no one the wiser, a testament to how many interesting things were going on at once. Tonight, however, he cursed it. Half of the whispers revolved around his rumored engagement.

Sebastian read his face.

"We can hide in the gaming room, if you wish," he suggested.

"My mother is watching me like the peak-nosed hawk that she is."

"Where do you think you got your nose?" Nicholas jabbed. "Dance with Miss Francis, Sebastian, so that Lennox can have a moment of peace."

Sebastian guffawed, steadying himself on a marble bust of some ancestor.

"I would frighten her to death," he declared. It was true. Sebastian was overly tall, his dark brown hair nearly shorn to his scalp, and he still had an excessive tan from his travels, which gave his skin an imposing leathery look. He cut quite a figure compared to the ghastly pale Englishmen who rarely saw the outside of a club.

Elias craned his neck, sweeping the room to find Miss Francis. Poor bird, she was just about as helpless to the fate of their marriage as he. She was being twirled about by a viscount of minor importance. In that case, it would not be until the next waltz that he must dance.

"Yes, let's escape to the gaming room for a spell."

The darkness and smoke in the men's-only room was a welcome respite from the bright ballroom. Nicholas peeled away from the room to peer over the card tables, looking for a worthy opponent. The two cousins found another corner to occupy. They were brought drinks immediately by Frost's observant staff, drinks much stronger than they would have gotten in the main room. Sebastian took a drink and exhaled happily.

"Oh, much better. Now—I am getting the impression that Miss Francis is not a love match, Lennox."

"Astute of you."

"In love with your mistress, eh?" Sebastian set his drink on a mantle and shook his head at Elias's censorious glare. "Come now, Nicholas told me, and you would have said so yourself soon enough. Are her stockings really blue?"

"Only at the club."

"Which, speaking of, I am quite bereft that you have not yet invited me to the Dove."

Elias grinned. "I am sure that Thackeray would agree with me on this account . . . we would like to keep our women."

"Len-nox," he groaned.

"In all seriousness, Sebastian, you only just returned. And now that Thackeray's bird is safely in a cage, I do not know how much time we will be spending there."

"What of yours? Safely in her cage?"

Elias drained the rest of his brandy at that sentence.

"She is not mine."

"The whole male segment of the *ton* thinks so."

"They should inform her, then," he said, feeling the bitter expression that pinched his features. "For I am having no luck convincing the harridan."

"Really now?" Sebastian's eyes danced. There was nothing he liked more than a little intrigue. "Even with the piano and the restored courtyard and the afternoon bath?"

"Gods, how do you know all of that?"

"I have my sources, Eli. You cannot possibly think that your actions have been secret. The staid and scholarly Duke of Lennox loses his wits over a lightskirt? They could not make up better gossip."

"Loses his wits?" Elias objected.

"Some say you have gone mad," Sebastian said pleasantly. "I love it. Makes you a trifle more noteworthy, like perhaps you are a human being after all."

Elias regarded his cousin with reproach.

"Come now," continued Sebastian, "you must admit that hunkering down at Oxford and building walls of books around you was a pointless activity."

"Right," Nicholas agreed, returning to the group to clink his glass with Sebastian's. "So very boring."

"There is part of me that agrees with you," Elias said.

"He has even been displaying a sense of adventure," Nicholas told Sebastian.

"No!" Sebastian put a hand to his heart in jest. "Impossible."

"I am a duke now," Elias said stiffly, "yet you two insist on still treating me as if we are at Harrow in the dormitories."

"And Nicholas will be a marquess and I will be an earl, what of it?" Sebastian said. "We are still the boys we were, which is perfectly fine. This woman makes you better, Lennox, and that is not something you will find again. You are a duke, as you said, so you can do whatever you want. Go get your girl. If your mother protests, send her packing for the dowager house in Scotland."

"I cannot do that." Elias paused. "But I want to do that."

"Gods, man. Get out of my house." Sebastian was grinning. "I am throwing you out of the party."

Nicholas turned him toward the door.

"I will yet again cover for you," Nicholas smirked, "if only to pay you back for the times you have poker-faced lied to my mother in order to save my arse."

"Josephine is not expecting me," Elias insisted. "It would be unaccountably rude."

"All the better to catch her off guard," Sebastian looked about an inch away from wiggling his eyebrows suggestively. "I will even dance the waltz with Miss Francis for you."

"Have a nice night, Eli," Nicholas pushed him forward.

Sebastian smiled at Elias with that same schoolboy mischief he had mentioned.

"My servants will bring your carriage 'round the back. Godspeed."

◆ ◆ ◆

As Josephine pulled on the garish blue stockings, the prevalent thought in her mind was that she would not be sad if she never had to put them on again. Elias's decisiveness was crawling into her brain, making her think that there was another way to help the girls of the Dove, and maybe she did not have to do it alone. Perhaps she would not need to don the stockings much longer, if Elias understood the gravity of the situation. She had resolved to speak with him, as soon as the moment presented itself.

After dressing, she went to the courtyard, yet another place in her life that the duke had changed. The careful redesign captured the moonlight in a soothing manner, and there was an aura of quiet. She could not guess how much Elias had bribed Mother to effect the renovation. Josephine sat down at the single table, surrounded by flowers that had been planted, and folded her hands. She was unsure of what she should be doing, other than wishing Elias were with her.

A voice cut into the still evening.

"BB," Digby croaked, strolling into the light. His ravaged features were not done any favors by the candles dotting the scenery. "Nice place yer fancy fella made here."

"I did not ask for it."

"No, I suppose you dinnit." He scratched his grizzled chin and appraised her from head to foot. "Such a huge amount of trouble from such a tiny little thing, you."

"Pardon me?"

His grubby hands were curling in and out of fists. She could not tell if it was a threatening gesture, or just some kind of tic of his. Digby was Mother's strong arm and not much else. None of the girls had ever been able to figure out if they were related or he was paid help, but he was unfailingly loyal to the woman. He had moved a little closer and Josephine shrank away from the odor that surrounded him, as foul as his heart.

"Little bluestocking," he growled. "You have become a thorn in our side."

"Digby," she blinked, attempting an innocent look to ward off his threat. She was never very good at the naive act, but she had to try. "Is this a joke? I do much for the Dove's customers; Mother has said so herself. I know I have been scarce lately, but—"

"But you are busy rutting the duke?" Digby leaned forward, breathing into her face. "Lucky 'im, gettin' you in the bag. I don't buy it, though. Think yer plannin' something. Think you 'ave been all along."

She tried not to flinch.

"I have no—"

Josephine did not even get to finish her sentence before he had grabbed her by the shoulders and hauled her to her feet.

"We ain't idiots, BB—or Josephine, right? Right?" He shook her. "Girls find shelter over the years, always right before we can sell them to the highest bidder. It had to be someone working here. Someone who knows the place."

"I try not to think about what truly goes on here."

Her calm façade was cracking by bounds. She should have taken Sally's warning more seriously. She should not have agreed to another of Elias's flights of fancy. Digby's giant hands tightened on her forearms, reddening the skin beneath.

"Stuck up little bitch," he snarled. "Don't know yer place, even in a whorehouse."

"Take. Your hands off of me."

She struggled, but it was soon obvious that she was outgunned. Digby's only true talent was brute strength and Josephine knew she could not match it. She was also not going to be able to goad him into a battle of wits. He exhaled a breath rancid with anger into her face. He had been given orders, and he would complete them.

"One thing for you to be all hoity-toity, but quite another thing for you to be hurtin' business." He unsheathed a knife from his belt, where he always displayed a few prominent weapons. She cringed as the metal touched her cheek. Her first instinct was to kick him, but he had pinned her against the wall so effectively, she couldn't move at all.

"So full of hope," he grunted. "Let's widen yer smile."

"I don't know what you're talking about," she insisted, barely moving her mouth, the blade was pressed so deep. "Please, Digby. Let me go. I will do my job at the Dove and you will have no trouble from me."

"The thing is, lovey," he said, twisting the knife a bit so that it glinted in time with a flash of his jagged teeth, "I know yer lyin'. I saw your bookshop, saw little Sapphire, put two and two together. Don't need to be no professor to do that. Just had to follow the duke and he led me straight to ya."

Everything she had feared was coming true. It sank into her gut that she was probably going to die soon. The freedom she had glimpsed now felt like a cruel joke.

"I have not . . . done anything . . ."

Josephine did not know what she could say to convince him. She barely cared. Her words were wisps that floated past her attacker's head and unwound into the night air, so little impact they made. She felt her muscles relax in a strange way, sagging and resigned to their fate. Her one coherent thought was that she would surely faint.

Digby's grinning face swam as he pressed himself into her further.

"Mother said I could have my way with you first."

She closed her eyes, knowing what was coming next. After that, she didn't care if he killed her. She would not want to live after that. He cupped her breast and his lips grazed the side of her face, leaving a wet trail. She braced for the inevitable onslaught.

Nothing happened. It was as if he disappeared. He was yanked back and the air in front of her was empty. She opened her eyes to see him crash against the wall beside her, Elias's arms locking him into place. The knife clattered to the ground.

"Apologize to the lady," Elias demanded, cutting off Digby's air with a forearm. Josephine had never seen such fury in the eyes of anyone before. Elias was incandescent with rage. "I said—apologize."

Digby sputtered words that must have been pleas for forgiveness, but they were unintelligible. He choked in futility. Josephine was also gasping for breath—she thought she might be imagining the duke, dressed to the hilt, but somehow managing to pin a thug to a wall, with little effort expended.

He turned his head, turned those fire-filled and frightening eyes on her.

"Are you hurt? If there is even a scratch on you, I will kill him right here."

Digby struggled, fruitlessly, and Josephine managed a dry smile. "I do not think that necessary."

"Fine." Elias sounded disappointed. He dispatched the thug by slamming his head against the stones with the perfect speed and pressure. There was a sickening thud as his skull hit the concrete. Digby sank to the ground, unconscious, turning into a heap at their feet.

"How . . . ? How did you . . . ?"

She felt faint. She tried to hold herself up, but instead found that she was supported by Elias's arms. His words came out on a rush of adrenaline and Josephine started to come back into awareness from the strange purgatory of panic.

"I've not just lessons in literature, love. Thackeray is addicted to boxing and I accompany him to Gentleman Jackson's on a regular basis. I thought it a pursuit that might come in handy. I am also quite an adept swordsman, but I do hope it does not come to that."

She burrowed into the warmth of his jacket. His heart was pounding beneath the thick fabric.

"I thought you had to go to Lord Frost's ball," she whispered.

"I left. Thank god I left." His voice was muffled against her hair as he held her head to his chest. "Are you really all right? Completely?"

"Shaken. Bruised. That is all."

"Gods, Josie. If he had hurt you—"

She looked up at him. "Thank you."

"We are going to Ashworth. You will broach no argument."

"For once," she smiled, "I will not."

❖   ❖   ❖

On the carriage ride back to his estate, Elias held her hand. She leaned her head against his shoulder and they were silent. Josephine felt a bit numb. She knew she should start telling him the whole sordid tale, but the silence was so comfortable and he was so warm, she could not bring herself to begin. They arrived at Ashworth Hall by way of the servants' entrance.

She watched through the carriage window while Elias dismissed more than half of the servants who had rushed to their master's arrival. She was whisked away by Dryden and his unreadable face, deposited in a room with a hot bath and tea. Josephine soaked for a quarter hour, digesting what had just happened. It was more than clear that she needed to confide in the duke. Still, she worried—how would he take it all, would he even understand?

She emerged from the bathroom, wearing a bathrobe she had found. The fabric was heavy and soft, absorbing the dampness of the bath as it enveloped her. It must have been Elias's—she was clearly in his private chambers. She did not think he would mind and it seemed ridiculous to put back on her costume. She never wanted to put it on again, in fact.

The door opened into his bedroom, where he sat hunched at his desk, scribbling something. She closed the door with what sounded like a deafening click and he turned. He dropped the pen.

"Good lord," he swore. "Look at you."

"I'm sorry," she said quickly. "Did you want me to . . ."

"Take it off? Yes. But not yet." He stood, crossing over to her. "I will not marry Miss Cecily Francis and I want the name of the woman I do intend to marry."

She did not like the look in his eyes. It was positively vulpine. Though there was but one candle burning in the room, the moonlight streaming through the windows made it just bright enough for her to see the evil he was onto: He was unbuttoning his jacket as they spoke. The light glinted off of his buttons and illuminated his sensuous, long fingers and their deft motions.

"You shaved this afternoon," she said, for lack of any other words. She was focused on his movements as he laid his coat and then waistcoat against a chair.

"I had to, but I am still the same unrepentant rogue." He had a sudden expression of concern. "Are you sure you are all right?"

"I am fine," she smiled, only a touch hesitant.

"Good." His cravat unraveled with one tug and he dropped it to the ground as he walked toward her. "Then may I tell you why I left Frost's ball?"

"I—are you undressing?"

"Yes." Elias took her hand and led her to his enormous bed, plush and expansive. They both sat and he bent down, unlacing his boots. They hit the floor with a thud and he faced her again, running a hand across her cheek.

"I left Frost's ball because all I can think of is you. Your laugh, your voice, visions of you squirming under me." His eyes flicked briefly to her lips and she shivered, though she was not cold in the robe. Elias no longer seemed uncertain, his every movement and all his words were quite decided. "You've taken over my imagination completely and it is . . . most vexing. I can abide it no longer. I want you . . . not just once, always. I need answers, love, so I came for them. I came for you."

The low voice he spoke in, dark with promises, was so sensual that he could be reciting Latin conjugations and she would feel it in her bones. He kissed her, first exploring, then deeply. When he pulled back, his eyebrows were drawn together sharply in the glowing light.

"If something had happened to you," he said, pain on his face, "I never would have forgiven myself."

He lifted her back to the headboard, not giving her a chance to speak. He trailed kisses along each expanse of flesh that was exposed as the robe shifted. When he spoke, he branded it into her skin. "But I also realized . . . that you are not a fragile woman. I have been too delicate with you. No more. You have no need to be coddled. I want your real name, darling, and I will have it tonight."

"Eli," she breathed, feeling helpless against his assault. After making the conscious decision to tell him everything, he was doing a good job of making her forget it all.

"Yes. How jealous I am that you have a name to groan."

He had somehow gotten her into a most vulnerable position and now his expression had lost any mischief. He knelt between her legs, untying his shirt with languor. His passion made him look dangerous, as if he would not be denied anything he wanted. She was transfixed for a moment, her eyes feeling greedy for the glowing skin of his tight chest.

"The robe, love. Shall I take it off for you?"

The matter was not up for discussion. She could not get her hands to move, so he obliged, untying the belt and whisking it from her frame. She watched it flutter like a leaf behind them. For a moment, she felt too bare, until she saw the look on his face. He had frozen, except for two fingers on his left hand, which traced her body, now open to him.

"Heaven help me," he murmured, his digits trailing across her nipples so lightly that she jumped beneath him. She had never seen the glazed look in his eyes before, as if everything else in the world had fallen away, his bed an island unto itself. His to plunder. He leaned into her again, kissing her until she felt deranged. The minute their naked skin touched, every thought flew out of her mind and was replaced with a sheer need that she could not even name.

Elias drew back again to look at her, expelling a breath that sounded frustrated. His hand wandered down her torso and her eyes shut of their own accord, the last image of him burned on her brain, his hair tangled and mouth quirked, bare chested but still in his trousers.

His fingers danced in a repeat of their performance on the settee, but now more unhurried and intimate.

"Keep your eyes closed," he said against her ear.

She tried to form a sentence, but it came out as *oh-oh-oh*.

His lips left her ear, following a map down her neck with lengthy stopping points at each breast and then the soft swell of her stomach, where his tongue made a remarkable appearance at her belly button. She gasped.

"Mmm." He smiled against her skin. "I will never give this up, my darling. Your face in passion—I mean to see it again and again."

His head moved down, nuzzling the soft curls that lay between her thighs. She realized she was holding her breath and clutching his arms, which were taut and braced against the bed.

"Across that piano bench," he spoke as he kissed the center of her pleasure, first tentatively, exploring as if the very notion of time belonged to him, "in a carriage, in a closet. My library, then your book-shop. I will exhaust you."

She felt his teeth on her inner thigh and had to hold back a most unladylike squeal. Shapes and motions replaced words and under his considered ministrations, a blinding white light began to build behind her eyelids. She felt as if she was rushing forward, but toward what, she did not know. His hands moved toward her bottom, supporting her and affording his mouth better access. She was shivering so much that she feared she would lift right off of the bed. Whatever he had her nerves chasing, it was getting closer with every flick of his tongue.

His hand covered her mouth as she climaxed, stifling the reflexive noises he had extracted from the breakable part of her, this desperate release of moans spilling into his palm. He pressed a cheek to hers as she gasped, the hard length of him straining against fabric and press-ing her sensitive core, so that she could not stop her hips from circling in urgency. She needed him inside, but he had stilled, smiling down at her with triumph.

She realized it was his name that she was panting: repeatedly, insensibly.

◆ ◆ ◆

It took all of Elias's self-control to not just plunge into her, but he called on reserves he had never used before, breathing as evenly as he could muster. She was his, he saw, her eyes had changed. The barriers she used as a defense collapsed into frantic little gulps of air and she could not seem to stop her pelvis from grinding against his.

He knelt back, still between her legs. He couldn't help the victorious grin on his face. She was still watching him, her hands tracing his chest in an anxious, impatient dance. He divested himself of his pants, trying to keep calm. It was not easy, not when he had been waiting so long for this.

"Darling," she whispered. "Come here."

Elias was happy to obey, wrapping a hand around the back of her neck to kiss her, taking his time to explore her mouth. He nestled between her thighs, painfully hard at her entrance. Every moment he spent kissing her, she grew more insistent. Her voice cracked against his mouth.

"Now," she pleaded. "Now, please, please."

"Soon," he said, staying as immobile as he could, while she shifted and came perilously close to taking him in. A groan broke out of his mouth, but still he hovered, just the tip of his shaft throbbing against her. She looked a bit frenzied.

"Elias, I want . . ."

"I want your name," he said. "Your real name."

"I . . . oh, I . . ."

He stared down at her, the eyes that seemed so sober in the light of day now blazing with heat. He moved his length against her, relishing the sweet torture and the way she bucked in need. She was magnificent and she belonged to him. He was hers just as certainly.

"My name is Elias Alistair St. Cyr Addison and I am the Duke of Lennox, and I have a lot of courtesy titles that I shan't make you endure now. I want *you*. Not Josephine Grant, not the bluestocking . . . you. Your name, madam."

She reached up and wrapped her hand around his neck, into his hair, drawing him into a measured kiss. He entered her with that movement, sheathing all the way to the hilt, and she arched with a whimper.

"Analise," she confessed hotly into his ear, as if the word were being wrenched from her. "But call me whatever you want."

"Analise," he repeated, lost to the feeling of her surrounding him, being inside of her. "Ana."

He muttered it into her neck, marking her with her name as he thrust forward, at first taking his time, teasing her with the slowness. Her fingernails clutched his back as he moved in her, gaining speed from his sheer need to take her. Her legs wrapped around his back as they fell into a rhythm, the same rhythm they had been weaving with words since they met. He sagged, burying his face in her shoulder, his hips rocking back and forth feverishly. He was unable to hold himself up anymore as he found his release, explosive and sightless, on the lovely sound of her true name.

After a moment, he sank back against the pillows, pulling her against his chest.

"And your surname?" he grinned, his breathing still not recovered.

"Do not push your luck," she whispered, wrapping more tightly around him.

"Just tell me, Ana, for goodness' sake, you know I will find out."

"Quail," she admitted.

"Analise Quail," he pronounced with satisfaction. "The woman I adore."

He felt her turn to peek up at him in the dark, but he did not open his eyes nor try to mask the placid smile he wore. He had an arm around her like a bolt of steel. He would not let her get away, he resolved. Frost was right, probably for the first time in his life.

"What is your middle name?" He opened his eyes a slit, showing her a line of glittering black amusement.

"Edith."

"Gads, horrible," he grinned, stroking her hair. "Does not suit you."

"Oh, what, Elias Alistair St. Cyr Addison is any better? Affected, dear."

"I am a duke," he sniffed.

"Are you? I had quite forgotten."

"Lovely," he exhaled. He scratched her back, unable to keep his hands from moving over her creamy skin. He relished the feel of their bodies against each other, with no artifice, and repeated her "new" name to himself like a mantra. "I would love to forget that I am a duke. You will feel the same when you are a duchess. I suspect you will hate it for a while, or no—come to think of it, there will be so many things for you to control that I would be in danger of losing you to management of the estate and ambitious charity endeavors. We should schedule an hour at the end of the day, before bed, for brandy and conversation."

"Elias," she said, sobering. "You must stop this nonsense."

"Analise," he growled back, loving how the effect of her real name shook her. "No more of this. I will sooner marry a goat than any woman other than you."

"In the afterglow of a tryst."

"In the light of day as well." He tightened his arms around her. "Do not cheapen what is between us. What do you think about moving to Oxford with me? After Alessandra makes her debut, of course. I really do not want my seat in bloody Parliament, spending the rest of my life arguing with old men. It is not unprecedented to give up the mantle. We may stay in London during the Season, but really we have choice of my estates. The one closest to Oxford would allow me to continue my studies and perhaps you could . . ."

"Eli," Ana said, pulling the blankets around her. He briefly mourned the sudden demureness, but then he saw the look on her face. "Stop. You are lovely, and that was lovely, but there is still . . . another matter we have to discuss."

"Yes, the matter of Mr. Digby and the Dove. I know you usually do not appreciate my meddling," he said gently, "but while you were bathing I took the liberty of informing your girls and Thackeray of the danger. I have put a watch on the Paper Garden. I do not think that Digby will be quick to retaliate, however, having been bested by—"

"—a duke," she finished. "I know. The advantage of your title will likely save my life."

She turned back to him, her heart absolutely in her eyes. It rendered his in half to see it. He held in a breath, feeling that she was about to let him in. Finally. *My Analise*, he repeated in his head like a mantra. She turned back to take both his hands in hers.

"Eli, what I am doing at the Dove, I have done without the benefit of a title. I gave up any ties I had to the nobility when my mother and I left for Scotland. When I returned, I took up the management of the Paper Garden, which was a gift from my father to his mistress. Her name was Josephine Grant. She had no family, and so it was fairly easy for me to pretend to be her heir, a touch more difficult to destroy the public records once I had convinced the solicitors that I was her daughter. What I did not know then was that my father had left a mound of debt tied to the Garden. Miss Grant had never been able to pay them off, but the writs still survived. When I began using her name, they found me. It was all I could do to keep my head above water when

I found the position at the Sleeping Dove. I did not want to sell my body, thought I could not, but playing the piano was a talent I acquired during the education of my youth."

Elias did not even move, afraid that it would stop her talking.

"My father—he was a baronet, I may as well tell you—dallied to the point of notoriety in Staffordshire. It ruined my mother's life and all of our reputations. At the Dove, I saw a parade of men like him, going through woman after woman with no regard for their well-being. I wrote the book. Every woman in the Dove has to rely on these horrible men to earn money for food and to have a roof over their heads. There is not another option available to them . . . so few are the occupations that women can pursue. What's worse, they have no hope of education by which to make their own ways in the world. Is this fair?"

He shook his head.

"No, darling. It is not."

"Writing the book did not seem enough. When I found out that Mother Superior was selling girls to groups of nobles, I started employing some of the ladies, so that they could cut down on their time at the Dove or leave it altogether. I taught some of them to read. They stayed with me until they could find some way to support themselves. If I had not given them shelter, they would have likely joined the ranks of the women Mother Superior sold to the highest bidder. I believe she is pawning them as pets, or worse, there are whispers that she used to deal with Dashwood's Hellfire Club. What she does—she *does*, Eli—is sell girls to peers who will pay to do whatever they wish with them. I cannot think too long on what happened to the unlucky ones."

His limbs were working now, so he pulled her toward him. Elias settled against the pillows, enveloping her, hoping that it was reassuring. In reality, he was burning with anger at Mother Superior and her atrocious business.

"They should not be able to get away with this."

"But . . . you know why, do you not?" She looked up at him, her gaze hard, as it must have had to be to endure all the years she spent at the Sleeping Dove. "You are a brilliant man, Elias, surely you do. The men that Mother deals with are—"

"Above reproach?"

"Precisely." She looked away. "I will understand if you must throw me over. I will not like it, but I will understand. Your position—"

He cut her off with a frustrated groan, tightening his arms enough to crush her against his chest.

"Stop that, Ana." Every time he said her name, it all felt more real. They could make it work, he knew. He was still euphoric, but the adrenaline from the whole evening was draining from his body. "I know it may not seem like it, but none of this is insurmountable. But now, we both need a good night's sleep. You can yell at me and make assumptions in the morning."

"We are safe here?" she fretted. Elias smiled and kissed her head, feeling immensely grateful that he was the one who could provide sanctuary for her.

"The safest you have ever been. And we are going to keep it that way." He smoothed her hair, while laying down and settling her into the crook of his arm. "I promise, we can fix this. Tomorrow. Right now, you are exhausted."

"I am," she yawned against him. She seemed almost as if she would lodge more protest, but after a few minutes, her breathing slowed. He stayed up long after, matching his breath to hers, meditating. And planning.

◆　◆　◆

She woke up for the first time in years feeling like Miss Analise Quail, which was unnerving to say the least of it. The daughter of a disgraced

156

baronet, penniless, unable to enter a room in Staffordshire without people whispering. She had thought that shame was over once she and her mother went to Scotland. Never again would she have to hear vicious gossip from the lips of vainglorious ladies, saying how her father had brought their family to ruin when he openly flaunted his mistress and then barred his own wife from his house. There was no way she could go back to it, the pinched faces of disapproving society ladies. Her eyes shot open upon consciousness, but the nightmare persisted.

She was at Ashworth Hall. She had slept at Ashworth Hall, in the bed of a duke.

The duke in question was already up and dressed, sitting at a small desk. Steaming tea and a half-eaten pastry sat near his elbow as he scribbled on a piece of parchment. He was so very *there*. Undeniably there, and so sure that everything would be fine. Even though his mother would never approve and the situation at the Sleeping Dove was irretrievable. She sat up, the gravity of the situation dawning on her. No matter how perfect the night before had been, she could not marry a duke. There was simply no earthly way.

"Good morning, Ana," he smiled, without looking up. He said her name in a maddening casual way . . . as if it was easy to say, as if he had never known her any other way, as if it wasn't loaded with the bitterness of her past. As if it could mean something different than it had.

A sob caught in her throat. He did not seem to hear, small mercy, and she swallowed the emotion.

"I have taken the liberty of arranging for a bath to be brought to you after we break our fast," he said, gesturing to a setup of food far more lavish than she was accustomed to, laid out on a sideboard. "I have been up for a few hours; there is much to be done. I will send an accountant over this afternoon to go over your books at the Paper Garden and—"

"What? No." She sat up.

He turned around and arched the imperial eyebrow at her, the one she found so nettlesome.

"Howsoever bad you think the damage stands, your finances can be fixed. Besides, once you agree to marry me, I thought we might expand the Garden. I will need to know where it stands presently to plan for its future. To plan for our future."

"No, Elias—you really have no idea of what—"

He crossed his arms, his eyes playful. "I will soon enough, Miss Quail." There was a different light in him this morning, a confident disobedience. "No argument will reach my ears."

Analise threw him an icy look, a rush of anger piercing her affection for him. Must he be so haughty? She wrapped the blanket around herself, seeing a dress approximately her size draped over the dressing partition. She slipped behind the divider, feeling both irritated and dismal.

She heard rather than saw Elias's valet enter the room, just as she slipped the dress over her head.

"Your Grace?"

"Yes, Dryden. Do mind that Miss Quail is behind the partition. Let us not be ungentlemanly, make it quick."

"Miss Quail, sir? The bluestocking?"

"I will explain later. Is there word from Miss Francis?"

"Yes, she will meet you in the park at half past."

"Smashing. And the cleaning at the Paper Garden?"

"Progressing nicely."

Ana scowled, deciding to stay put. His generosity was making her feel embarrassed, like he was rescuing a damsel, and she resented it. She would have survived, she told herself, without this man and his resources. She had just hit a snag and she would have been fine. His meddling had actually made things more difficult for her. The lobby of her shop would be sparkling if she had not wasted so much time parrying with him. And he was going to meet Miss Francis! Of all the nerve!

"Are you all right, love?" he asked, as the door closed behind Dryden.

She must have lost track of time in her building fury.

"Fine," she snapped, reemerging.

"I was thinking—I should like to reprint *On Society* with your proper name when we marry," he said, dusting the parchment he had been fussing with. "This is a letter requesting special license from the Archbishop, but it should not take more than a few days. When would you like to meet my mother again? We had best get it out of the way forthwith."

She found that she was staring at him, openmouthed. He was really going through with the utter fairy tale that he spouted the night before. He meant to marry her. Not as a ruse to tup her, but in reality. He stood, caressed her cheek so tenderly that the anger drained out of her. It was quite remarkable the hold he had on her, which in turn made her angry all over again.

"May I remind you," she said in measured syllables, "that I never agreed to wed."

Elias pulled her into his arms so quickly that she gasped.

"You will. I've made an appointment for you to see a modiste this morning. Sally will meet you there. I, however, must inform Miss Francis that I cannot marry her. Then, I have some plans to put into motion in regards to the Dove. I thought you and I might spend the night at the Paper Garden, have dinner alone."

"Elias," she said weakly. "Are. You. Mad."

"Mmhmm," he agreed, tilting his head to kiss her. He reached behind her for his overcoat and hat, planting a final kiss on her forehead. "See you this evening, dearest."

CHAPTER NINE

"Though you may not believe it, dear reader, I do not find fault with the institution of marriage. If both parties feel well-matched and are able to choose a partner of their own discretion, I cannot see opposing a union of equals. There are very few comforts in this world and I would deny you none. For myself, I doubt it is a particular comfort I shall attain."

—FROM *ON SOCIETY'S ILLS AND THE REAL PRICE OF PROSTITUTION* BY JOSEPHINE GRANT

Elias jumped down from his carriage, still buoyed by everything he had put in motion upon waking. He thought if he could make arrangements quickly enough, Miss Analise Quail would not have time to over think, analyze, or refuse him. He would be far more comfortable if she did all that nonsense after they were safely wed. The sooner she was an acknowledged duchess, the easier it would be to deal with whatever spectre remained of her father's checkered past.

"Miss Francis," he called, waving his hat in the air. He realized he must look flushed, ridiculous, so unlike his normal contained visage. He no longer cared. He liked how he felt under the grip of this "madness" and would deny it no longer.

"Your Grace," she smiled as he bent to kiss her hand. "You are in a fine humor this morning. I was so glad that you contacted me. It is far too long since we have had a chance to speak in private."

His eyes glided over to her chaperone.

"Oh, Agatha. She does not count. She would never betray my confidence."

"Shall we take a turn about the park, then?"

Elias offered his arm, straightening to return to more of a ducal distance. It would not do to make her think that his happiness revolved around her presence, as he was about to tell her that it did not. He felt a bit like a cad—Miss Francis was as helpless in this business as he; she had not chosen him. He really knew nothing about the slight blond woman, beyond the fact that her father was an earl and their families approved of the match.

"Miss Francis," he began tentatively, when there was enough space between them and other early morning strollers.

"Please, let me speak first. I do not want to marry you."

He could not hide his look of surprise, but hoped that his jaw was not hanging open in an uncivilized way. The bald statement shocked him. He glanced sideways at her, his mouth forming into a strict line as she continued.

"With every due respect, Your Grace, do not ask me to marry you. We are ill matched. There is no spark between us except the politeness that our families have bred into our veins. I will happily sit at a table with you, be social, etcetera, but I do not want to wake up in any of your houses every morning. We have nothing in common."

"Pardon me?"

It was the only phrase that he could force out.

"You must feel the same, correct? I think we have been used as pawns, for my part. Your mother and my father, both widowers, seem to get along smashingly. A rumored engagement between their children was a convenient excuse for them to spend time together. Did you not realize?"

"No, I . . ." he stuttered, fumbling for words. "I have been preoccupied."

"I noticed."

She smiled and for the first time, Elias could see a woman beneath the front she presented to society. The poor girl simply had the disease common to London society females—personalities hidden beneath layers of proper conduct and silly rules. It was unfair to compare her to his Ana, his wild and untamed Ana, who had flown in the face of everything that Miss Francis had been raised to respect as gospel.

"You are in love," she said, squeezing his arm. "I thought as much. But the waltz with your cousin confirmed it last night. Lord Frost told me that you are entranced by a bluestocking. He says that you are a good man, but cowardly."

"Cowardly!" he exclaimed too loudly.

She laughed.

"I only think that he meant in regards to telling me your true feelings."

"I was going to tell you today!"

"I know I may seem like a delicate flower, Your Grace, but you would be surprised."

"Hence the sly grin you wear, which I have never seen before."

"You did not give me the chance," she returned. "But it is no matter. We have weeks behind us in which we could have been friends to make up for now. I will tell my father that I refused to marry you. You may tell your mother that I am obstinately against our union. If it is not too forward, perhaps you should also tell her that your heart is otherwise engaged? I hope that when you settle with your new duchess, I shall be invited for dinner."

Elias felt a sudden rush of affection.

"Of course," he said earnestly. "We are indebted to you."

"There is one thing," Miss Francis said as he pressed her tiny hand between his palms. "When you have me for dinner, do invite your cousin."

◆　◆　◆

Analise felt like she had no choice but to be carried away on the wave of Elias's planning. Her whole day was laid out before her, including a carriage, chauffeur, and imposing footmen who looked suspiciously like bodyguards. Before Elias left, he poked his head back in the bedroom door and whispered, "Stop worrying."

Stop worrying? She did not think she could exist without the worry. In fact, as she picked at the breakfast that a pleasant but jumpy maid brought, Analise found plenty of reasons to be vexed. By the time she finished her tea, she was sure of two things: that she loved the Duke of Lennox and that she had to leave for Scotland.

She would meet Sally at the modiste, and then make her plans when she returned to the Paper Garden. If she was quick, she would have enough of a head start that Elias would not be able to ascertain her departure in enough time to follow her. It was cruel, and he deserved better, but he had left her no choice.

She loved him. Truly.

This horrific revelation carried her through her morning, followed her to meet Sally. Her friend was already at the dressmaker's, in high spirits and miles of fabric.

"Analise!" Sally exclaimed brightly, dropping a bolt of dazzling blue that would be far too daring for day wear. It was strange to hear her real name from the mouth of the woman who had known her the best over her years in Cheapside, though she had only known her as Josephine Grant. Analise's eyes darted around involuntarily, thinking that Digby and Mother could be after her at any time. The footmen were standing just outside the door, much larger than normal servants, courtesy of the duke's heavy hand. She was torn between feeling grateful and ashamed.

"You do not mind that I call you by your proper name, do you?" Sally said in a lower tone as she approached. "I would find it silly to continue on with a charade when I know it all now and you shall be the Duchess of Lennox soon."

"Do keep your voice down."

Analise pulled her friend to the side, lowering her own voice.

"I want to apologize to you—I should have told you long ago that I was not who I said I was. You do understand that I had to protect myself, don't you?"

"No, not really," Sally smiled. "I think you have a proclivity to make everything more difficult than it should be. But I do not love you any less. What do you think of this?"

Sally held up a pretty floral pattern that suited her perfectly. Analise nodded in a numb way.

"The proprietress of this establishment is quite attentive, as our beaus have instructed her, and we are to pay no attention to price. Do you see anything that may fit you? I am certain Lennox would love to see you in something fine this evening. I believe he has an important question to ask." She wiggled her eyebrows.

"Oh, Sally," she sighed. "I can never accept this kind of generosity, nor should you."

"Speak for yourself, spoilsport. I mean to let my Nicholas lavish me with gifts."

The dressmaker glided up to them with a welcoming smile.

"Miss Quail," she bowed her head slightly. "It is good to meet you."

Analise was distinctly uncomfortable with strangers uttering her surname.

"I am Amelie Lacroix, though you may know that." Her lilt was a giveaway to her nationality even before she introduced herself. Her store was the very height of fashion and delectable French gowns were all the rage—for ladies. Analise did not consider herself one of the soft women who could lounge in those gowns. How would anyone get anything done, corseted and laced everywhere?

"His Grace has chosen a particular frock for you, my lady," Miss Lacroix continued, "and I might add that his taste is impeccable."

She led the way to the back, to the more expensive looking fare, leaving a trail of strong perfume in her wake.

"*Et voilà!*" Miss Lacroix said with a flourish, presenting a dress form. The gown on it was a stretch of the imagination—Analise thought it so beautiful that she was surely making it up, not seeing it in front of her. It was a deep burgundy color, ruching on the skirt, and elaborate beading—done by hand—featured on the bodice. It was a confection that would likely cost a year's salary at the Dove.

"Heavens," Sally murmured.

"His Grace thought it would be a perfect fit, but you must try it on. My girls will help you."

"I—"

Analise only got out one syllable before the shopgirls had shuttled her behind a dressing curtain. She could feel Sally's smirk radiating all the way through it. Miss Lacroix began chirping happily with Sally about her own gown orders and measurements, all the while the assistants fluttered around Analise, adjusting this and lacing that. Once again, the duke had placed her in a whirlwind without her permission. She wished she could flee.

The girls turned her to the looking glass and she was taken aback. She did not look like plain Josephine Grant at all anymore; she looked like Miss Analise Quail, respectable society daughter. But even more— she looked like she could stand next to the Duke of Lennox and make quite the pretty picture. It was tempting to let her fancies run wild. How would he react when he saw it? Would he like it on her?

Sally burst behind the curtain, her curiosity getting the best of her. She stopped in her tracks, her mouth open in a delicate "o." It was an extremely odd expression.

"What?" Analise demanded.

"It's just that . . . you look like . . ."

"What?"

"A duchess. You look like a duchess."

Analise pursed her lips and examined her face in the looking glass. The worry lines that creased it, hovering above the outrageous expense of a dress, did not speak of a duchess. She looked the part, but inside . . .

She may have appeared a duchess, but she felt a fraud.

◆　　◆　　◆

After Hyde Park, Elias returned to Ashworth. He said a silent prayer that Dryden had been able to get his mother out of the house. The entryway was free of people and he could hear servants bustling in the kitchen, probably preparing a light lunch. He handed his overcoat to a butler without a word and walked toward his study, staying on the carpet in case Sophia did happen to be about. He felt like a teenage boy, sneaking around, planning outrageous schemes. He smiled to himself.

Alessandra was waiting for him in the hallway, hand on her hip.

"Well?" she asked expectantly. "I know you didn't actually feel ill at the party; I wheedled it out of Nicholas and Sebastian. They're downstairs waiting for you, by the by."

He sighed and continued past her.

"You three are the worst sort of hens—pecking and pecking."

She followed him to the library. "You are grinning like an idiot," she said, "so it must be good."

"Close the door, Allie." When she did as he asked, he continued. "I believe I will be married by the end of the week, but not to a certain Miss Francis."

Alessandra clapped her hands together happily.

"I positively knew it!" She kissed his cheek. "I am so very happy for you both."

"No time for happiness just yet," he said, settling down behind his desk. "Many loose ends, some of which I cannot go over with you."

Her brows shot up in offense.

"However, there is something very important you can do for me."

Elias leaned back to reach the nearest shelf, which held the copy of Ana's book that he had first read. The book he had cursed, then accepted and understood, then cursed again as its author drove him to his limits—now there was an opportunity for the blasted thing to be used to his advantage.

"Can you see to it that mother reads this? I think that if she does, it will go a long way to convincing her that I have chosen a well-suited wife."

"Josephine's book?"

"Her name is actually Analise, but that is an unfinished story that I shall have to tell you later."

"How am I to make mother read?" Allie nearly whined. "She values my opinion on nothing at all."

"I have faith in you," he smiled. "You are clever. I am sure you will find a way."

She reached out for the book, but he pulled it back.

"On second thought, I shall give you a new copy next week. I have some edits that need to be made, and I shall write an introduction."

"And I am to explain that to Mama . . . how?"

"Just say she is an author that was recommended to me and I admired her work so much that I offered to write the introduction for a new edition." He waved a hand. "I do about a dozen of those kinds of introductions in a year, though neither of you are interested enough in my work to read them."

She rolled her eyes. "How you suffer, dear brother."

"Well? Will you help?"

"Of course I will." She turned to leave, but turned back once more before her exit. "But you owe me," she warned.

◆　◆　◆

The accountant arrived just as Elias had said, in the midst of the chaos the Paper Garden had become that afternoon. Sapphire was doing her level best to direct the army of liveried footmen that had arrived in the duke's carriage. The carriage—crest, shiny lacquer, and all—had the neighbors in a perfect tizzy trying to peek in the windows. For her part, Analise had drawn the curtains and hung the Closed sign, as much as it pained her to lose potential business. She could not accept customers in this state.

"Miss Quail?" The bespectacled accountant, stuffed into his suit, approached her with a notebook clutched to his chest. He looked decidedly uncomfortable with all the activity around him. "It is quite a busy day in your store."

"Mr. Tavisham, yes?" She ducked a feather duster wielded by a tiny woman whose name she did not yet know. The accountant looked from side to side and then his eyes settled on Analise. They stared at each other for a beat and every passing moment, Analise became angrier and angrier with the duke. He had not even asked if she wanted to be invaded and now her store was overrun with people. She had not told Sapphire yet why these people were calling her by a different name and the horror was sinking in that she would not be able to hide any longer. How was she going to transition from being plain Josephine Grant back to Miss Analise Quail, who was evidently destined to be a duchess? All of this agitation, with a few minor strokes of Elias's quill, and he still had not rightly asked her if she wanted any of it.

"Do you find His Grace to be annoying?" she asked Mr. Tavisham.

"My lady?"

"What about meddlesome? Infuriating?"

"I beg your pardon, madam?"

"Plainly, do you find the Duke of Lennox to be irksome?"

"Miss Quail," he repeated her cursed name in a shocked manner. "I find His Grace to be an upright and fair-minded man."

"He has you all fooled," she said under her breath. "He is a rotter."

"Did he not tell you that I am here to look at your ledgers?" The man's eyebrows knitted together with confusion.

"Of course," she said, shaking her head, which did nothing to clear it. Sapphire rushed passed her, sputtering something unintelligible, pursued by three footmen carrying wobbly stacks of books. "Please, Tavisham, follow me out of the pandemonium."

Analise wound her way to the rare books room, which doubled as her office. It was the place where the first edition of her book had always been, until Elias had bought them all. He had invaded every area of her life. Even walking in the room made her think of the way his mouth had widened when he looked at her and said *"Blue"* in that drawl of his. It was the room where they had first looked at each other unmasked, where he had drawn his lips across her wrist. She remembered the way he looked at her then, the delighted trouble in his eyes.

"Miss Quail?" The accountant intruded into her reverie.

"It is cramped," she apologized in a wisp of a voice. "But all of my records are on the corner shelf behind the desk, arranged by year." She was shocked at herself that this was happening, that she was actually letting the man look at her finances. It was beyond a breach, but she was beyond resisting Elias's pushiness any longer. In point of fact, she did not want to at all. Damn the persistent bastard, there was just no helping it.

"I am to specifically note the debts and their sources, so that we may start with a clean slate. Is there a bell here that I might employ to summon someone in case of questions?"

"Pardon?"

"Am I not being clear?" He arranged himself in front of the ledgers, speaking as if she was already supposed to be gone. "I will begin with the debts, as the duke has requested them closed, and I will ring if I have any questions."

"The duke is paying my debts?"

Mr. Tavisham looked up, exasperated.

"My lady, he seems to consider them as his own debts as well. Are you not Analise Quail, his fiancée?"

Her stomach dropped. He was telling people this without even asking her. Would he ever bother? Did he just assume her compliance, like any of his other servants?

And the more disconcerting question: Would her answer be yes?

◆　◆　◆

"And so there we are," Elias finished, crossing his arms and studying Nicholas and Sebastian. They lounged in his sitting room, both now looking at him dumbfounded.

"Let me summarize to the best of my ability," Sebastian said. "Your bluestocking was actually raised in respectable society, some scandal made her and her mother flee to Scotland, she returned with a chip on her shoulder against the peerage . . ."

"And men who dally," Nicholas added.

"And men who dally, and then she got a position at a whorehouse where she wrote a book decrying the system."

"Indeed," Elias confirmed.

"And *then*," Nicholas continued, after pausing for dramatic effect, "the avenging angel began to help the wounded doves around her, making a poor financial situation worse."

"A regular martyr," Sebastian smirked. "I do not like the type."

"We should not forget that she was also operating under a surname. Nay—two surnames, one at the Dove and one at the Paper Garden. And now her nefarious employers are onto her scheme and they may attempt to get rid of her. The whole thing is quite theatrical, Lennox."

"Yes, Thackeray, yes. It is all very epical. I am sure you are pleased to no end that I have to deal with a situation that I would not believe if it was written in a ridiculous novel."

"Rather like a play," Nicholas agreed. "A farce, even."

"It is wonderful," Sebastian said. "It is, in fact, delicious. This story is deserving of a hero."

Elias frowned.

"Oh, stuff it, Frost. This is not a story. This is my *life*."

Both of his friends stopped for a beat, looked at each other sideways, and burst into laughter.

"The tortured, lovelorn Duke of Lennox!" Nicholas struggled to continue through the laughter. "The stone-faced statue is felled by the crusading beauty!"

"Do tell any playwrights you may know," Sebastian snorted. "They could not plot it better than that."

Elias looked up at the ceiling in exasperation.

"If only there was someone to write you two out of the tale."

Nicholas stood up and clapped him on the back.

"You would not change it." He poured brandy for all three of them. "Do not ruin our fun. We have waited almost twenty years to be able to tease you for not thinking logically. To deny us this little comfort would be cruel."

"He speaks absolute truth," Sebastian said. "You did not let me off lightly the time that I stole Lord Welles's carriage to take the barmaid from the village to a carnival."

"Or when I lost every shilling I had, and then some, on a bet that I could steal the headmaster's day journal from his chambers without reproof. That particular act of bravado was born of a desire to impress his daughter's governess."

"That was a fool's errand and you knew it," Elias muttered.

"We could go on," Sebastian offered.

"Save your breath; I take your point. Do consider, though, that while you jest, a business proposition hangs in the air."

Sebastian set his glass on the table with an authoritative clink.

"You want to buy the Sleeping Dove."

"All of us," Nicholas clarified. "He wants all of us to buy the Sleeping Dove."

"As with most business ventures, it is sensible to pool resources so that no one person shoulders all of the responsibility."

"*There* is the trusty logic again." Sebastian leaned back into a chair.

"I maintain that it would be profitable for all involved. And Frost, you are doing nothing in London since your return, so why not? It would give Nicholas a reason to spend more time here, as well, and less with the overbearing marchioness," Elias reasoned, hoping that they would not continue ruminating for long. The truth was, he could do it himself but he didn't want to. He had spent the majority of his existence lifting responsibility on his own. The thought of drawing his two closest friends into a venture that would require working together was vastly appealing. As annoying as they could be, they were his family. He found that after all this time, he wanted his family around him. He wanted to be among them, not trapped in a tower alone with the weight of the world on his back, like some tortured fairy tale prince.

"Surely you do not want to continue selling girls." Nicholas's eyes looked far away for a moment. It was obvious that he was thinking of his Sally. "It is not right; it was never right."

"No, but I thought perhaps gambling tables would make the same amount of money. Those tables need able bodies to attend them."

"The lovely ladies go from the beds to the bar," Sebastian filled in. "They bring the drinks and provide sparkling conversation, making for a pleasant place where it will be quite easy for the gentlemen to forget how much money they are spending. Yet—you cannot be blind to the fact that there will still be transactions for . . . a little extra entertainment."

"Not our business," Elias said. "Their choice."

"Lennox." A note of warning entered Sebastian's voice, which was bizarre to him. Sebastian's smooth tones were generally employed to charm and Elias was not used to the teasing overtones disappearing completely. "As much as I would love to support you in ruining yourself, this would be a terrible scandal."

Nicholas had an entirely opposed look his face: ideas were quite visibly flashing across his brain.

"We would not be public owners, Frost. Do not be silly."

"Exactly," Elias said, tapping a finger on the table to avoid looking at Sebastian.

"And who is your figurehead? You both evidently have this all worked out already. Forgive me for having just returned from traveling, I do not know the history here, and am at a disadvantage in it. Nor am I so blinded by love that I am willing to stake my fortunes on it."

The smirk had returned to his voice.

"Sally is the figurehead, of course," Nicholas said. His voice rang with pleasant surprise. "It is rather neatly tied up. Impressive, Elias."

"Well?" Elias asked. "What say you?"

"I will give it some thought," Sebastian hedged.

"I am done thinking," Nicholas gave a wide smile. "I am your proud partner."

"All right. Fine." Sebastian sighed a long-suffering sigh.

Elias felt himself grin. He stuck out his hand to each man in turn and they shook. Sebastian punctuated the transaction in his incomparable way.

"This will end badly, but I am certain it will be interesting."

◆　　◆　　◆

Analise returned to the Paper Garden feeling shell-shocked. The dress that made her feel like a duchess would arrive later; it needed minor alterations, but Elias apparently expected her to dress for dinner. She had not done such a thing since she was a teenager. It seemed ridiculous. The Paper Garden had undergone even more changes since she was gone, including two intimidating guards outside of the front door. Mother Superior would not dare try anything now.

Sally had gone back to her posh flat and Sapphire—whose real name was Georgina—was having lunch when Analise walked through the door. Georgina was very young, only nineteen, and she had taken to the bookstore gratefully. It allowed her to quit the Dove and oversee the cleanup of the place. She did not ask many questions, but Analise suspected she thought that the duke had ridden in on a white horse to save them all, which needled her pride. But, since the explanation was far more complicated, she chose not to discuss it.

"Hello, Miss Grant!" Georgina said brightly.

She also chose not to discuss the issue of her name.

"Good afternoon, dear."

"We've been so busy! I had to lock the door in order to eat."

"That is wonderful," she said, as flat as the covers of the books surrounding them. It was wonderful in a sense, but confusing in all others. She would never be able to give up the way that she lived—revolutionary ideas and all that went with them—and the duke did not seem to realize that she was dooming him to a life of scandal. The downfall and humiliation of the duchy of Lennox would be on her head. If Elias expected her to become a respectable duchess, he would be a sorely disappointed man.

"I'll reopen now," Georgina said hastily, folding her napkin. Analise became aware that she had probably been silent longer than socially acceptable.

"Finish your lunch," she said, waving her hand. "I am not displeased with you; it has simply been a trying day. Thank you for dealing with this upheaval."

"Thank *you*, Miss Grant. I cannot express how happy I am to be here."

"Do not mention it," Analise said. "I will be in my room. My head is throbbing."

"Do call if you need anything."

She nodded and ascended the staircase as if she were dragging her body in a sack. She was tired in her bones. The spiral, in most instances a comfort, seemed like an unnecessary complication. She tried to lie down to clear her head, but she was restless. Elias would return that evening, still under the impression that she was amenable to a union between them. There was no more time to stall about making a decision: she had to either tell him she was leaving or give in to being swept off her feet and into a different life.

She heaved a traveling chest out of her closet and flipped the lid open. She was a woman who liked to be prepared, so she began to pack even though she was not sure it was truly her wish to go. Her doubts about their relationship were so deep that she had not even expressed them to herself. She had been selfish; she wanted every moment with him until she had to admit that she could never be his wife.

She emptied the contents of one of her drawers into the chest, folded summer dresses that she had not been wearing. Some were so old that they were covered in patches where they had been mended over and over. She added her jewelry box to the pile, what little baubles she retained. She had only kept her mother's favorite pieces and family heirlooms; the rest were pawned long ago to pay the bills and help the girls.

She stopped, stared at the inside of the luggage—what was she doing? Elias deserved better than her running away. In the same breath, he deserved better than attaching himself forever to a woman that would shame his family.

She opened an armoire to pack her warmest clothing—as she remembered Scotland, it could be heartlessly cold. It would be a fitting exile. She had not meant to toy with the duke, but she had let him believe he could construct a happy ending. Analise had known from a very young age that the nobility would never accept her and that fairy tales were just that: fairy tales. She stood with a pair of boots hovering over the chest, thinking. If she were to leave, she could not tell him; it would not work. He would not let her.

She sat down at her desk and began to draft a good-bye letter, which kept coming out all wrong and consisted mainly of scrawls and strikethroughs. She would rewrite it later, if she made the decision to leave.

By late afternoon, she had packed all of her necessities and covered them with a sheet in a corner downstairs with the insufficient letter, but she had still not come to a decision about whether she should stay or go. The tower of chests stood in memoriam to her indecisiveness and the unanswered question that had taken root in her heart.

❖   ❖   ❖

Elias had wrestled over whether to take a pistol to the Sleeping Dove to confront Mother. He was not afraid of Digby; he was fairly certain that he could best him again. Frost and Thackeray would be with him as well, so his physical well-being was more than safe, it was assured. The gun might help with intimidation, though.

In the end, he did not bring it. He did not need anything except his righteous anger at the hideous woman who called herself Mother Superior. Part of him hoped Digby would give him a reason, even a tenuous one, to beat him within an inch of his life.

It was exhilarating, taking action like this. He had never been very proactive, choosing to mostly stay out of others' affairs. He had always been the exact opposite of Thackeray in that regard and compared to Frost, he was a prude. Now, standing outside the door of the Dove, he realized that the things he had done since meeting Analise far surpassed even their stupidest escapades.

And he loved it.

"We are just walking in?" Sebastian asked, peeking around the back of the building. "Why not something more heroic, like going through the courtyard to employ the element of surprise?"

"It is a place of business, Sebastian. We are walking in."

"It does not seem dashing or dangerous, Elias, you must admit."

"I know they love me here," Nicholas shrugged. "I have spent a fortune on drinks and on Sally until she left. Furthermore, I am not Lennox. I am not the troublemaker."

"You took away one of Mother's girls," Elias reminded him. He opened the front door and began making their way to the back. "I think it would be best if we just went in as if we were still patrons, mingle until we can secure a conversation with Mother."

"And what if she will not talk to us? You did knock her lackey unconscious."

"She will talk."

"I still think it would be more dramatic to climb the courtyard fence."

"Shut up, Frost."

Elias opened the door to the Dove, but Digby's arm was across the entrance. Behind him, they could see the sparkling piano, a monument to the money Lennox had already thrown the way of these odious villains. The room was empty of both customers and girls.

"Yer Grace. Been expectin' you."

"Good evening, Mr. Digby," Frost said from Elias's shoulder. "I am Sebastian Frost, heir to the Earl of Harrington. I have heard much about your establishment."

"We're closed," he said gruffly. "Repairs."

"I need to speak with your boss," Elias said without much inflection.

"She don't need to speak to you."

"Digby, my good man," Nicholas said in a loud, jolly voice, "I doubt Mother Superior would pass up the opportunity to have a conversation with three handsome, wealthy men."

"I simply must meet her," Frost added with a dramatic flair that bordered on silly.

Elias would have thought they planned it, it sounded so casual. He saw Mother's lumpy form appear behind the bully, her neck craned to take in the three peers.

"Let them through," she barked. "I assume you have a good reason for coming back here, Your Grace? Your bluestocking's not here, if that's what you're looking for."

"I know where she is." His eyes darted over to Digby. "And she is very well protected."

Mother put her hands on her hips.

"Talk fast, Duke. My time is money and you have wasted quite enough of it."

"It has come to our attention that girls have gone missing from your establishment. Considering that Digby just assaulted the bluestocking, I think you know why we are here."

Digby hovered behind Mother Superior, lurking with menace.

"I'd be happy to go another round," he snarled.

"Watch yourself," Elias warned. Digby put a foot forward as if he was about to make a move. Nicholas and Sebastian stood up behind Elias, flanking him. Elias waited a beat before he continued. "Let's keep this civil. I have a proposal for you both that will be beneficial for everyone."

"Sounds familiar," Sebastian muttered to Nicholas.

"Oh?" Mother could not hide the greed in her voice.

"You can't be listening to him," Digby said, nearly whining. It made Elias suddenly certain that this man was the madam's son. "He knocked me cold against a stone wall!"

"It was less than you deserved," Elias spat. "Must I repeat the performance?"

"Lennox," Thackeray interjected. "You should let one of us have a go. It is not fair for you to have all the fun."

"Do you want to take our money or not, Miss Superior?" Elias asked mildly.

"Money?" Mother's eyes glinted.

"There she is," Thackeray smiled. "There is the girl we know."

"Hardly a girl," Frost mumbled.

"Yes, money." Elias slid a piece of parchment across the table, the amount the three had agreed to offer. It was more than generous. Mother's eyes widened as she read it. Digby looked over her shoulder, then cast a suspicious glare at the trio.

"I considered going to the authorities," Elias continued, "but I reasoned that you likely have connections in high places. Those bastards who pay you to hand over your girls are certainly not untitled men. Litigation would be a mess. So, I have enlisted my two friends here in order to give you an offer—take this generous amount, board a boat, and do not ever set foot in this country again. Sign the deed of this cesspool over to us."

"Why?" Digby spoke again, as the woman had fallen into a stunned silence.

"Lennox likes things tied up neatly," Thackeray said, "and Frost and I like to gamble."

"Also, he would not let me kill both of you and bury you at Ashworth," Frost added in a disturbing deadpan.

"We will accept this offer," Mother said, after feigning consideration.

"But—"

"No, Digby. I am tired. Let these boys ruin their reputations or burn the place to the ground, I do not care. I want to be comfortable."

"Reasonable," Nicholas said. "Everyone wants to be comfortable. It may be the one thing that unites us all."

"Do not orate," Elias reprimanded. "Your answer is yes, then?"

"I said so, dinnit I?"

It was strange that the first thing that came to Elias's mind was the fact that the courtyard now officially belonged to him and Analise.

"Excellent," he said, clapping his hands together. "My solicitors will contact you tomorrow with the details."

The two crooks were still agape, Digby disbelieving the ease of the transaction and Mother dumbfounded by her luck. Elias looked to his friends, sure that his face also betrayed him. There was not a word to describe how brimming with hope for the future he felt.

"Gentleman, shall we?"

"What a disappointing confrontation," Sebastian commented on the way out. "I expected fisticuffs. We do not even get to climb the fence upon exit? Not very theatrical at all."

"It is your fence now, Frost," Nicholas shrugged. "Climb it any time."

◆   ◆   ◆

Analise paced the front room of the Paper Garden. She had put the burgundy gown on, because Elias had chosen it, but as the hours stretched she felt more and more ridiculous. It was difficult to complete any task of worth in the tight confection. She felt useless in the confining bodice, even though there was really nothing to do . . . an army of ducal servants had made the store sparkle. Georgina told her, before leaving for the evening to visit with Sally, that she had seen more customers that day than the whole total of her time at the Garden.

Dryden made an appearance to deposit two covered dinners at the front table. He had set up a center of operations for the duke, from a tiny nook near the history section. The valet was mostly silent, except for a brief greeting and a comment that she looked lovely.

She felt awful. She still did not know if she would stay or go.

Two short knocks sounded at the door before Elias opened it. His eyes scanned the room for her and in that instant she saw that he had dressed for dinner, too. As if she was someone important. Her heart twisted. This was a man from the world she had left behind and now she would have to leave it again. The exquisite cut of his jacket, the feathery hair that framed his face, the crispness of his collar: He was easily the most gorgeous creature she had ever seen. He was so flawless that her only thought was how much she would like to disassemble him.

She stepped out into the light.

"My god, Ana," he said when his eyes found her. His mouth was ever so slightly open and that particular glaze had come over his tawny eyes. "How will I make it through dinner without ravishing you?"

In her inspection of him, she had forgotten that she was wearing the gown he had chosen. They moved closer to each other like they were spellbound.

"I was thinking something similar," she returned. He grabbed the back of her neck and pulled her into him, which was not something she resisted. "Thank you for the gown."

"Entirely my pleasure," he smiled, his curved lips a thing of the devil. "It has comforted me to think of its existence all day, imagining it on you, imagining it slung across a chair upstairs after I've liberated you from it."

She actually blushed.

"Behave," she said without meaning it.

"Whyever would I? Things are finished between Miss Francis and I. My mother is less furious than she would have been because Lord Francis has asked her to the opera. I no longer have any reason to pretend I am not pursuing you." He kissed the side of her mouth, lingering. "Avidly pursuing you."

"The food is getting cold," she said, though it was a pathetic attempt at a protest. His nose was on her neck again, a moment before she felt his tongue on her ear. She began another sentence, something about how the food had already been sitting for a while, but its meaning was lost. Her body relaxed into him without consent of her brain.

Some minutes later—she could not quantify how many—they found themselves tangled together against a desk. Elias pulled out of a kiss, proud with dishevelment, and let out a long breath.

"Well, love," he said, "I must admit that you were right to remind me of dinner, because I am going to get carried away rather quickly. If we do not eat now, I fear it will go to waste."

"Oh," she said, having forgotten about any dinner. Once he started kissing her, her vocabulary was whittled down to words like *oh* and *god* and *yes*.

"Besides," he continued, taking her hand and leading her back to the table. He pulled out her chair for her. "I have had a very eventful day that I need to tell you about. When I take you bed, I do not intend to do much talking."

There was that shiver again, that instant reaction to him for which she could find no logical explanation.

"My day was packed with activity," she commented, straining for an informal tone. She lifted the silver lid of her dinner, releasing the steam trapped inside. "I own new dresses for the first time in years, courtesy of a handsome duke. Then I came home with a careful guard of devoted servants, also courtesy the handsome duke. It makes me feel ludicrous, Eli."

He poured wine into her glass, pursing his lips in reprimand.

"Dearest."

"Please do not be patronizing."

"I am not. You are being intractable. Once we are settled, you can choose however many attendants you wish to have, or none at all. But right now, we had to think of the very real danger you were in. Were, in the past tense. You are safe now."

She sighed, picking at her food.

"Years of careful work, obliterated in under a month. All of the girls who counted on me . . . I let them down."

"Not so," he protested. "You have saved them. It is done. We are now the proud owners of the Sleeping Dove, along with my esteemed friends Thackeray and Frost. Do you have any ideas to rename the place?"

"What?"

"I was thinking something more masculine, since we intend to make it into a gambling hall. Or something French."

"You bought . . . the Dove."

She could not believe she was saying that sentence. It echoed in her head. His contented smile stabbed at her—he truly thought he was going to be able to fix everything and provide a happy ending.

"If you want to be technical," he shrugged, "I bribed the villains."

He began eating, watching her with a satisfied gaze, considering the case closed. He took a sip of wine and turned to her, putting a hand on her leg impishly.

"Not hungry, love?" His long eyebrow shot up, lightning across his forehead. "If you are not, I would rather be in bed."

"I just do not know what to say. I have already accepted so much of your charity, but this is beyond my imagination. It is objectionable."

"It is not charity. I should be offended by that," he frowned. "I love you. It is selfish. I love you and I want to see you happy, so I am using my resources toward that goal."

To hear the words so frank from his mouth made her emotions lurch forward and obliterate the doubts in one whoosh. He loved her. The conviction in his voice was unwavering. She could not possibly leave him. She must have been mad to even consider it. Things were already starting to work themselves out. Elias loved her—he said it aloud, brazen and unashamed. He said it like a simple fact. She let out a breath she had not realized she was holding.

She kissed him so fast that he was startled.

"Could you . . . Eli, did you say you love me?"

"Of course I do, is it not obvious?" He looked so adorably confused that she let out a burst of giddy laughter.

"Thank goodness," she said.

"And?" he prodded, squeezing her hand.

"And what?"

"And in these sorts of situations, the other party also declares their truest devotion to ease the mind of the brave soul who has laid his heart open."

She felt playful, examining his expectant face.

"I expect I do love you. It seems I must. I cannot shake you even though you are an awful lot of trouble. You are smug and dogmatic."

"True enough."

"But I suppose I love you."

"How generous." He picked her up in one unbroken motion and she wound her arms around his neck. "I shall make you pay for that. I shall make you say it, over and over again."

"Always threatening," she nuzzled.

"It is a promise. You will not be able to say anything but *I-love-you-Eli-I-love-you*."

When all the candles in her room had been extinguished, he proved that he was nothing if not a man of his word.

◆　◆　◆

Elias woke up in a smashing good mood. He and Analise were alone, except for the guards outside of the Paper Garden, so he pulled on his breeches and went to search for tea. He whistled to himself, finding that being shirtless and barefoot in the bookstore was the most at home he had ever felt.

Dryden was off to check on Nicholas and Sally, who would be lunching with them that afternoon. They all needed to get started on plans to reopen the Dove, which would be quite the project. Even more so now, as they would be planning a wedding at the same time.

But first, Elias smiled to himself, he would give Ana the ring he had in his dinner jacket and ask her if she would be his wife. He was excited. He knew she had no idea he would even ask; he was sure that she thought he would just plow through without appropriate permission.

He would do it as soon as she woke up.

He opened random cupboards, searching for tea leaves. They had to be around somewhere. A pot boiled on the fire, whistling softly along with the duke. Where would they have put the tea? He opened a few more drawers in a rather offhand manner, and then something caught his eye.

It was a letter, on top of three suitcases, which were packed to bursting. It was Ana's handwriting and it was addressed, more or less, to him. The page was a mass of scrawls and crossed out sentences, but as he scanned, the meaning became clear. He forced down the void that opened in his stomach and read it back.

My love,

Dearest Elias,

Lennox,

By the time you read this, I will be far enough gone that it would not do to

Please do not trouble yourself coming after me.

No one has ever been so good to

It seems not enough to say thank you for all that you have done, you must know how much it meant. I am in love with

Here there was a giant scrawl, a cloud of ink spirals, where her quill had come down with frustration.

I hold you in a most high regard. This is why I have gone away to Scotland and why I will not come back. There will not be a day that I do not think of you and please do not hate me. I hope that you will realize, perhaps not today or even tomorrow, but eventually, that this is for the best.

The loss of you is acute to me already, though I should not say it.

I will always wish you well.

Love,

With all my heart,

Fondly, AEQ

He stared at the sheet, not sure if he believed his eyes. His hand shook once, a tremor. She was leaving him. She intended to leave him. Yet she had let him believe the night before that all would be well. Not easy, no, but it would be well. Elias braced his hand against a counter. Had she let him go through with all of his plans, when she knew she would just leave him in the end? After all that he had done? His body temperature went abruptly from ice cold to running hot.

His fist curled, crumpling the letter. He cataloged in his mind the list of insane lengths he had gone to in order to win her over. It was shameful. No wonder Thackeray and Frost had been laughing at him. Everyone but him had been able to see how silly it was. He had wasted his family's money on a decrepit building that had previously been a brothel, wasted his time chasing after an impossible woman, to the point of neglecting his own duties. He had even involved his sister in the sordid ordeal. What sort of fugue had he been in, what sort of grip of heedlessness?

Elias's feet were already carrying him back to her chambers. Every part of him was on instinct alone, his precious logic blotted by hurt and anger.

Ana was just waking up as he reentered the room. She smiled at him from a haze of sleep.

"Good morning, my darl—"

"Going somewhere?" he demanded, shaking the parchment. He released it and it fluttered to the blankets. A look of horror crossed her face when she realized what it was.

"Eli, no—I wrote that bef—"

"How shoddy, you could not even be bothered to hide it." He yanked his shirt from where it had landed the evening before, draped on a lamp.

"I had not made up my mind. Stop, Eli, please let me explain—"

He snatched his cravat from the edge of the canopy and stuffed it in a pocket. His words were coming fast now.

"You were going to leave me with a letter? I think you capable of many things, Ana, but cruelty of this caliber? I do not even merit being told to my face that you have no faith me. You were going to run like a coward."

He stopped buttoning his waistcoat to glare at her. Her hands curled around the coverlet.

"I was, but I came to my senses." There was an anxious tremor in her voice, a quaver that he swatted away. "Please sit down, we should—"

"Oh, you did? Did you? Came to your senses?" he demanded. "What *are* your senses, Ana? I cannot tell the way you vacillate back and forth—you love me, I am a cad, you adore me, I am the embodiment of the evil high society. I am through with it. I do not care if you have come to your bloody senses. Did you ever have one bit of respect for me, or are you just laughing behind my back?"

He laced his boots enough to walk while she was still trying to untangle herself from the sheets. She reached out to him, but he shrugged her off.

"No, love, stop—you don't understand, I was wro—"

"I find that I am out of patience. I am out of tricks and out of options with which to prove my sincere devotion. I . . . am bloody exhausted." He plucked his jacket from a chair and retrieved the ring box from an inside pocket. He fumbled, so angry that he was shaking. His shoulders slumped, ashamed of his outburst, but too deep in it to stop. He threw the ring box at the bed, where it landed in a puff against the pillows with a gasp of deflation.

"It is a ring. I was going to ask you to be my wife, but I suppose I have my answer now. Do keep it. It will bring you a fortune if you pawn it."

He slammed her bedroom door, then the staircase door, then the front door. He was still pulling on his jacket as he stalked out of the Paper Garden.

CHAPTER TEN

"It would seem that a certain wealthy heiress is no longer looking over her fan at the D. of L. and the cracks are showing in the Uncatchable's façade. One need not look further to see the classic signs of a man with a broken heart."

—FROM A LONDON SCANDAL SHEET, APRIL 1832

Two weeks later, Lennox was part owner of the Sleeping Dove—though Thackeray was running the particulars and Frost had already claimed a room of his own—and the count of copies of *On Society's Ills and the Real Price of Prostitution* he possessed had ballooned to one hundred. The fifty new editions were printed with Analise's real name. He had also written an introduction to publish in the papers; that had been intended as an engagement gift. He resented all of this, but felt it a fitting reminder of the mistakes he had made.

No one asked him about Analise and he certainly did not mention her. Society at large thought he was brokenhearted over Miss Francis. Nicholas sometimes looked at him wet-eyed, as if he was about to say something, but he never did. Since leaving the Paper Garden and its owner behind, he had become a very effective estate manager. His mother was pleased, but her new generosity of nature had more to do with the courtship of a certain Lord Francis and less to do with Elias being a good son.

At least someone was happy.

Dryden knocked on the door.

"Your Grace, the gardener says the flowers are planted on the East Grounds. He wants to know if there will be anything further this week, on top of his normal duties."

Elias handed over a stack of papers.

"Yes. These are the plans for the West Grounds and they should start immediately."

The valet was silent for a moment, studying him sideways. Dryden had been with the Lennox family since before Elias was born. That being the case, one look from the valet could send the duke right back to his childhood. The particular expression Dryden wore now was a common one: not quite a reprimand, more of a scolding. As in, *You very well know you are doing something wrong.*

"If I may speak freely, sir?" he asked.

"I have never expected you did not, Dryden, so." Elias put aside the paper he had been reading. "Go on."

"I think it may be best if you retire to the country seat for a time."

"Do you now?"

"Rather, the house staff is overworked with your endless demands and sudden renovations. It may be easier for them to meet the goals if you are not changing directives at such a relentless pace."

"Hmm."

"Moreover, sir, I am concerned for you personally. There have been three letters from your Miss Qu—"

"That will be all, Dryden."

He blinked once and turned without hesitation to exit the room.

Elias would not tolerate the mention of her name. He could not tolerate it. It was like a curse on his head, that name. Of course, it could have been avoided if he had not pursued her. Hindsight was no particular comfort.

He had not read her letters, but they were good for one thing—rolling into cylinders that fit into the necks of empty wine bottles to hurl into the fireplace. The smell of burning parchment and ink was particularly satisfying if one drank late into the evening.

Elias started down the hallway. He had taken to eating luncheon on the terrace so that he could watch all the projects he had set in motion at Ashworth. It was also a way to avoid his mother until dinner and thus avoid making himself presentable until then.

He slowed, hearing his sister's voice from one of the rooms. He stopped in his tracks when he heard what she was saying. She was reading something very familiar, something that sent ice shards through his veins.

"And the problem inherent in this is that it would not be an extreme effort to bring equality to the sexes. It would not take anything away from the gentlemen to allow ladies into their classrooms, lectures, even clubs. Can you imagine what contributions our sisters might—"

Elias flung open the door, furious. Alessandra gaped at him, sitting as she was with his mother and a group of ten rather shocked ladies.

"Hello," he said, strangled.

"Duke," Sophia said in a smooth tone that indicated her annoyance. Of course, his mother was there; destiny would not have it any other way to assure his absolute mortification. "What is the meaning of this?"

"Eli?" Alessandra stood.

He could actually feel the sheen of sweat begin on his forehead.

"Yes. No. Pardon me," he apologized to the group, taking his sister by the elbow. "A moment, dear sister?"

"Ouch, Eli," she rubbed her elbow as the door closed. "I am only doing as you asked. What has gotten into you?"

"You are reading her . . . her . . . her . . ." He could scarcely force the words out of his mouth. "Reading Miss Quail's book to a gathering of socialites!"

Alessandra beamed with pride.

"It is a brilliant plan, if I may say so. You said to get Mama to read it, and here we are, at the first meeting of the newly formed Ladies' Literary Salon."

He turned his eyes to the ceiling.

"Damnation."

"Do not swear. If you did not want me to complete the task, why did you not say so?"

"I forgot."

"You forgot!" she laughed. "In any case, Mama does indeed like the book, most of all the parts about men being afraid of women's intelligence."

"She would," he groused. "You must choose another book. I apologize that I did not tell you sooner."

Alessandra crossed her arms.

"But we must finish reading and discussing."

"Fine, but understand—there is no point. Things between M-Miss Quail and I are closed."

"There is a point," Alessandra snapped, flouncing her skirts. "It is a good book and you are a *beast*."

It seemed that even if Elias resolved to cut Analise out of his life, she was intent on ruining it.

◆   ◆   ◆

Analise, having decided that a third letter would be pathetic, directed a glare at her packed luggage. She had seen no sign of Mother Superior since the damned duke and his friends had paid her off. Analise thought it still might be better to flee to Scotland. Every moment she spent in London was a moment she regretted her actions. Now that she was free, she could not bring herself to leave.

Sally, through Nicholas, told her that Elias was displaying a decided lack of patience for the mention of her name. She could not have mucked it up further if she had been actively trying to sabotage herself, which she had been doing unconsciously, anyway. The beautiful sapphire ring Elias had thrown at her sat on a high shelf, with one of the notes that said "*Doesn't matter*" propped up against it.

For someone who valued her own intelligence so much, it rankled to be proven such a superb idiot.

The bells above the door signaled a customer, which was happening more often these days. It would die down when the local gossips discerned that the Duke of Lennox would never be present at the Paper Garden again.

The false smile Analise wore for the public melted away the instant she saw Dryden at the counter. She nodded her head with an awkward jerk. She had been expecting this.

"Dryden. Good afternoon. I thought you might eventually be by to retrieve the ring—it is surely a family heirloom. It is lovely."

"My lady, no." He had a strange look on his face, almost pained. "A letter."

Her heart leapt into her throat and lodged there, until she saw the handwriting. It was not the duke's. She looked back up at Dryden, naked disappointment in her eyes.

"Lady Alessandra," the valet explained. He opened his mouth as if to say more and snapped it closed again. "Good day, Miss Quail. It was nice to see you."

"Good day," she said to his retreating back.

There was no pride in the speed with which she tore into the envelope.

Miss Quail,

I know it is too bold of me to do this as we do not know each other well. I hope that you will forgive the intrusion and not think me crass. Dryden tells me that E. did not read your letters. I am sure you are aware of how stubborn he can be. I will not beg you to come and speak with him in person, but I want to offer an excuse to do so. I have enclosed an invitation to speak at my new Ladies' Literary Salon. The other two pages are from an introduction my brother began writing for your book before you parted ways.

Yours in hope, Lady A.

Postscript: I feel I should admit that my aim is self-interested; E. has become a terrible bore, more than before if you can imagine.

Analise smiled at the last sentence. The first enclosure was a formal invite for "Miss Analise Quail, author" to speak at the Ladies' Literary Salon held at Ashworth Hall. The other was a sheaf of paper in Eli's script that was labeled "Introduction to *On Society's Ills and the Real Price of Prostitution* in Second Edition."

She only got a few paragraphs into the essay before she was crying.

I wish it was simple to dismiss the words in this book. In fact, my own life would have been much less troublesome if I had not made the acquaintance of Miss Analise Quail. However, I know that if I could turn back the clock to the moment I met her, the only thing I would change would be the speed at which I told her how much I valued her above anything else. It is not enough to shelter and protect a woman, as many of you assuredly think. One must also allow her to effect change in your life as you do in hers. Miss Quail, from the beginning, changed me in a positive light, brought things to the surface that I would not have on my own. She could not have done that if we had played by the constricting rules that society imposes, and I wager that we will be happier than most readers of this introduction could ever envision. I do not mean this as a boast. I mean this to spur you to action, to make you realize that you aspire to the wrong things. Noble blood and a seat in Parliament will not hold your hand when you are ill; your vast estates will not comfort you when you age. Three things will comfort you and the last is the greatest: art, music, and the quick wit of a beautiful woman.

It was a stinging reminder of the man she had lost. Now that she had known the Duke of Lennox, she could not imagine her life without him. Two weeks had done nothing to dull that pain; it had only worsened it. She knew she would never find another like him.

She sat down to write to Alessandra, to tell her that she accepted the invitation to speak. It was her best and last chance to make things right.

◆   ◆   ◆

Elias was not informed of Ana's lecture at Ashworth until the morning of her impending arrival. Alessandra told him of the visit in a very no-nonsense tone.

"Miss Quail will be coming to speak to the Ladies' Literary Salon this evening. Will you be dining with us?"

He was struck quite dumb.

"What?"

"Mother says that 'what' is a rude word, and you heard me."

"Miss Quail?"

"No, Elias, the king—yes, Miss Quail." She looked exasperated. "Will you be dining with us or not?"

"No," he said, lifting a paperweight aimlessly and setting it back down. He stacked his ledger and some papers neat as a pin. He arranged the quill pot, blotter, and a stack of envelopes into a neat triangle. "No, please send my regrets."

"Truly, Elias?" Alessandra put a hand on her hip to emphasize the force of her indignation. "Truly? Miss Quail is going to be in our home and you will not see her?"

He came out from behind the desk, stalking forward to force her out of the room.

"I said *no* and I do not appreciate your meddling. Next time you invite a guest for dinner, you should damn well inform me."

He slammed the door, his breath coming fast. Ana was going to be in his house. *His.* House.

"You are being unreasonable," his sister said from behind the door.

"Go away, Allie." He laid his forehead against the wood until he heard her footsteps patter down the hallway. There was a soft knock soon after.

"Your Grace?" Dryden asked.

"I am fine," Elias said, not opening the door. "Thank you."

It would not take a studied observer of human nature to see that he was not fine. His fists had clenched without his knowledge, his fingernails carving out mean red lines in his palms. He closed his eyes to fume. This was his fault. He should not have taught Alessandra to manipulate the affairs of others, but he had set a horrible example with Analise.

His brain went into a panicked whirl. He would dress for dinner, even if he did not plan on attending, for Ana would certainly try to seek him out. He pushed down the part of him that thrilled at this. If he saw her, his best tactic would be to ignore her. Ignore her with a cool and haughty air, calculated to enrage her. If she pressed him, he would pull up and say, "Get out of my house before I have you forcibly removed." The thought of saying this was satisfying. Every bloody day he wished that she would just go to Scotland as she threatened to in the vile letter that was still emblazoned in his memory.

In the hours that ensued, he changed his jacket thrice and had two glasses of brandy—not too much, not too little. He needed courage. The household outside of his study was bustling in preparation. If Dryden's lips had been pressed together any tighter, they would crack.

"Will you greet—er, the author—this evening, Your Grace?"

"No."

"Shall I ready the carriage, in that case?"

"No."

"And if the lady asks after you?"

"I am far too busy."

Contrary to his declaration, he was sitting behind his desk, placid as a duck. Dryden's eyebrows rose, but he did not elaborate.

"Very good then, sir."

A half an hour later, he heard a butler announce Ana's arrival from his post prowling in a parlor near the entryway. One might call it blatant eavesdropping, if one was looking at it from the outside. He preferred to call it investigation. He had to be prepared with the harridan in his house.

"Miss Quail," Alessandra said, radiating warmth. "We are so pleased you were able to come."

"It is an honor," Ana said. Elias could see her through the tiny crack he had left open in the door.

"My mother, the Duchess of Lennox."

Ana curtseyed.

"You look familiar," Sophia said, eyeing her sideways. "Are we acquainted?"

"Not exactly, Your Grace. You came to my store, the Paper Garden, once. With your son."

"Ah, yes. That is it. Your store is very dark, my dear, you should invest in oil lamps. Dryden, pray tell, where is the duke?"

Elias's valet snapped to attention, his eyes darting to the crack in the door. He was not the only one who spotted Elias, it seemed, for Ana's eyes had also found his in an electric charge.

"I am certain he is far too busy," she said with a secret smile. Elias was frozen to the spot. "May I see the room where I am speaking?"

"Of course," Alessandra nodded.

As the group started walking, Ana leaned closer to the door. He could almost reach out and touch her. There was a mischievous gleam in her eyes.

"Who is the coward now?" she whispered.

◆　◆　◆

Analise did not think she would be able to keep her wits together. Between seeing Elias peering at her, the sheer enormity of the estate, and the intimidating bearing of the duchess, she had to resolve not to flee.

She was numb as Alessandra showed her the library, but she managed to make polite conversation. As soon as Sophia left to dress for dinner, the younger girl broke out into a genuine smile.

"I really am so very happy you came," she squeezed Ana's hand. "Dryden says that Elias refused to come out of his study, but I do not think that will last long. I do wish you could have seen his face—"

"That is more than enough, Alessandra."

Elias was standing in the doorway, as he was wont to do. The way that man inhabited doorways was a criminal offense.

"Were you lurking, waiting for Mama to leave?" Alessandra accused.

Ana took in the welcome sight of Elias, having imagined his form in her mind every day. The weeks had seemed much longer than two. He did not look as happy to see her, however. He looked malevolent.

"If you would be so kind as to give us privacy," he said to Alessandra.

"Scandalous," she chirped, brushing past him. "Scandalous!"

She swept out, giggling, but she closed the door behind her nonetheless.

"How are things at the Dove?" Ana asked, thinking it a neutral way to start.

"At the club that I bought in order to please you, with which I am now saddled?" He did not come further into the room, skulking at the threshold. "It is fine. Nicholas and Sally are taking care of the change-over. Have you not spoken to Sally?"

"I have. She says that you are not involved."

"I am not. I do not want to go back there."

"I waited for you, you know. The first five nights after you, Nicholas, and Frost sent Mother packing, I waited there. Did you read my letters?"

"I have no taste for fiction at the moment."

"Then you would have been pleased with their veracity, had you deigned to read them. I was honest about the fact that I have been most unfair to you."

His face shifted, but only for a blink. It reassembled itself right back into a mask of displeasure.

"Oh?"

"Would you like me to enumerate the ways in which I have wronged you?"

"I would like nothing more."

"I treated you unkindly when all of your actions marked you as an honorable man. I let you go to insane lengths to prove your devotion, even though it was clear as day. I kept secrets. I distrusted you at every turn. I fought you when you were not waging war. Shall I go on?"

"I do not believe you are finished."

"I used your station as an excuse to hold you at arm's length and your gender as a tool to doubt your character. It is exactly what you did not do to me."

"I had not thought of it that way," he said, bemused. "But yes. Yes, you did."

He drifted nearer to her. Nothing had changed about the magnetism between them. When they were alone together, they gravitated toward one another. Her heart jumped. He touched her face and she tilted toward him. There was no reservation in her manner.

"I assumed you wanted to be my savior, not my partner," she confessed, "and I was wrong."

"Ana, I—"

The door flew open.

"Mama is coming back downstairs," Alessandra hissed.

"Were you eavesdropping?" Elias asked.

"Irrelevant," she clipped. She turned and called down the hallway with a burst of youthful exuberance.

"Mama! Eli will attend dinner after all!"

❖   ❖   ❖

Somehow his attempt to push Ana further away from him ended with her beside him at the expansive dinner table. The guest of honor at any function was always seated next to him. It was a special torture to escort her into the room, seat her, and pretend all the while that they were only acquaintances.

His mind was spinning on what she had just said. He had apologies of his own to make and hope began to bloom again. If they were both willing to admit the folly of the past months, perhaps they could make an honest go of it. Neither of them had given the other an especially fair shake.

The members of the Ladies' Literary Salon assaulted Ana with questions throughout the meal. *Isn't it all too shocking? Do you think these ideas will be welcome in polite society? Whyever did you begin thinking this way?* When there was a lull, Elias could not help but chide her.

"Miss Quail, I wonder if you worry what men will think of your book?"

"I do not worry what rational men will think, Your Grace. I worry what artless louts will think."

The whole table laughed.

"Too bold by half," the duchess said with sudden austerity. The table went quiet for a moment; no one wanted to disagree with a duchess.

"But I quite agree with Miss Quail on most counts," she added.

There was a visible loosening of the crowd and Alessandra let out the breath she had been holding.

"I am flattered, Your Grace," Analise said. "I was most eager when I received the invitation to speak with Lady Alessandra's salon."

The duchess began chattering on a new subject, some very urgent sounding list of reasons why the Countess of Spencer's garden party was sure to be fairly seething with debauched fripperies. Elias took the opportunity to murmur to Ana while the rest of the table was focused on Sophia's outrage.

"Your dress is very becoming," Elias said.

"I thank you, Your Grace," she lowered her voice to match his and turned her eyes away discreetly. "I am glad you like it—you bought it."

It took a physical effort to stifle the smile that tugged at his face.

"Do you play the piano, Miss Quail?" he inquired with exaggerated politesse. Half of the table had become interested in what a duke could possibly have to say to a female writer.

"All accomplished ladies do," she answered, "though I am out of practice. This past month has been . . . somewhat of a whirlwind for me."

Elias's foot found hers under the table. Ana made a delightful sound of surprise that she covered by clearing her throat.

"Intriguing!" the second daughter of a viscount across the way exclaimed. "Have you been having an adventure since writing the book?"

"An adventure would be an understatement, Miss Everly." Elias was impressed that Ana was remembering everyone's name, as the introductions had been short and chaotic. "The past few months have been utterly life-changing," Ana said.

He could not help it; he grasped her thigh lightly under the table. She smirked.

Alessandra was pontificating about something, which took attention away from the pair. Elias returned to the side conversation.

"Tell me again how wrong you have been," he said.

"Must I?" She smiled, closing her hand over his under the table. "It was difficult enough the first time."

"I do not know if I can forgive you," he said, trailing a finger along her upper thigh, smooth against the silk of her dress. "I may have to punish you. I have a few ideas for suitable—"

"Lennox!" Sophia barked from across the table. "What *can* you and Miss Quail be talking about?"

"I beg your pardon, ladies." He cleared his throat and attempted to regain control of the conversation. "I was merely telling Miss Quail how much I liked her book. I was remiss to not share it with the whole table."

His mother narrowed her eyes. She was unconvinced.

"In fact," Elias continued, standing with his wine glass. Perhaps a toast was a better way to divert attention. "If you would allow me a moment to toast our guest and thank her for coming to speak to the salon." He raised his glass. "To Miss Quail, that her bravery may be a lesson to us all."

"Here, here," Alessandra smiled.

Her sentiment was echoed. While glasses clinked, he caught Ana's eyes, smoldering at him under long lashes. She must have liked the toast, for she was looking at him as if he were something delicious. He could not help but return her gaze. A hot place opened in his chest and he felt how much he had missed her physically. It was something he had been trying his damnedest to forget.

The table around them returned to normal conversation, so he thought it was safe to murmur to her. He leaned and spoke as low as he could, out of the side of his mouth.

"We need to finish talking. There will be twenty minutes before you speak, will you meet me in the sitting room? Take a sip of your drink if your answer is yes."

She picked up her glass and smiled at him over the lip, a promise that he felt in secret places. When he looked away, still smiling, he saw his mother looking at him with suspicion. Nothing ever slipped by her.

"Shall we go through?" the duchess asked rhetorically, standing and throwing down her napkin. Chairs scraped all around as the guests followed suit. "Lennox, do you not think you should retire now? The ladies can hardly feel comfortable listening to such perplexing new ideas with a duke in their presence."

He rose, not averse to be rid of the group.

"Indeed, ladies," Elias bowed. He took the opportunity to kiss Ana's hand, since it would be acceptable in parting. "It was a pleasure to dine with you, Miss Quail."

She flashed that sly smile again.

"Good evening, Your Grace. Your hospitality is unmatched."

◆   ◆   ◆

"If you would excuse me for a few moments," Ana said, as smooth as she could manage after the impious looks Elias had been giving her. "I must collect my thoughts before I speak. Is there a quiet room I may use?"

"There is a sitting room near the entrance, m'lady," Dryden said, scooping her out of the copse of ladies. It was obvious to Ana that he had been given orders from Elias. "I will take you there."

"No longer than twenty minutes!" the duchess called after them.

"Do not be unwise, Miss Quail," Dryden whispered once they were outside of the room. "It does not befit the future mistress of Ashworth Hall."

"Shush," she said as he closed the door behind her.

Elias was so close that she could not even draw a breath before his lips were on hers. She returned his passion with eagerness, no longer with the doubt that had been in her kisses every time before. Something had shifted, unmoored in her. She could not deny that she wanted him with all her heart, in wanton ways and practical ways, day and night. Almost losing him was far scarier than the life-threatening situations she had faced on her own.

"This is perhaps a foolish risk," she said against his ear.

"What will they do if they catch us?" He gave her a look of mock horror. "Make me marry you?"

◆　　◆　　◆

"That would be the respectful thing to do."

"I respect you," he said darkly, grazing his teeth and tongue over the lace that framed her bosom. "Shall I take you upstairs and respect you over and over again?"

He pulled her into one of the cushy chairs and they sank together easily. She wound her arms around his neck, sideways in his lap.

"Are you still packed for Scotland?" he asked, dotting kisses up her neck.

"The trunks can go elsewhere," she said, bringing his face to hers again. She looked him square in the eyes, something that she had often been afraid to do. She had no fear of them any longer, and she was rewarded with his mesmerizing, shadowy gaze. "Here, perhaps? After we marry, if you will still have me?"

"I am considering it," he said, his mouth quirked sideways. "I may find it in my heart, my generous and noble heart, to forgive you."

Ana's heart sang with the jest—if he was bantering with her, he had forgiven her. She raked a hand through his hair. She must stay presentable, but there was no reason she should not take advantage of him. Even more so since he was being incorrigible.

"Do take your time and consider it."

"I have already taken too much time. I should have dragged you to the altar the night we met and sorted it all out later."

The retort she began was lost to his embrace.

"It has been a long two weeks," she groaned against him.

Perhaps it was the relief of having him back, or the extra wine she had at dinner, but she was emboldened. She had missed him in every sense. She had already told him how sorry she was, but he deserved . . . more. Something unthinkably indecent, right before she had to give a lecture. Even the thought of that did not deter her. It excited her.

She ran a hand down his breeches, gradual and wicked, the strain in the front jumping at her touch.

"Ana," he growled, "we cannot . . . actually. Not now—"

"Is the door locked?"

Ana slid off the chair, running her hands down his thighs as she knelt beside him. She savored his sharp intake of breath and the fact that he could not keep his eyes off of her. She took her time exploring his powerful legs, the taut energy of his muscles. She parted them at the knee and knelt down. He did not stop her, but his voice came out strangled and intense. His head lolled back in the chair.

"Yes, it is locked, but—you cannot do this—"

She tugged at the band of his breeches, just enough to reveal his hip bones, which she traced with her fingernails. He closed his eyes and his head sank back fully.

"You are really making a valiant effort to stop me," she replied, putting her lips to his stomach. She feathered kisses on the patch of hair below his belly button. He shuddered. She felt a moment's hesitation, for she had never actually done this before, though she had heard enough talk to be convinced that she would not embarrass herself. She felt powerful, seeing the way he was plastered to the chair. She loved that she could inspire that kind of desire in him.

"I *should* stop you."

It was a wisp of a sentence, barely even there.

"You should," she agreed, yanking his pants down further and taking his length in her hand. His forearms gripped the chair. She flicked her tongue, experimenting, and his arms tensed further. There was something so erotic about the way the veins came out in his forearms. She let her hair fall over his stomach as she leaned down.

"Ana—really—I cannot take th—"

She took him in her mouth and he stopped talking, collapsing into what sounded like nonsense punctuated with moans. She teased him with her tongue as she moved her mouth up and down slowly, trying to find what degree of speed tortured him the most. He had stopped protesting. His dark eyebrows were drawn together as if they were painted sharp across his forehead.

"Shhh," she scolded, drawing back. "You will give us away. Am I doing this right?"

He laughed, a short burst of disbelief.

"Yes, my lady. Oh, yes."

She let her fingers wander as she put her head back down to his groin, and he shivered when she touched the smooth planes of his skin. She was as fascinated by the exploration as she had imagined. She planned to do everything she had fantasized about in their time apart, everything that she had promised herself she would do if she got him back. It would take a lifetime to discover him. His breath was coming fast now, his bliss stifled into desperate whimpers filled with the fear of discovery.

"You must—stop," he pleaded, grasping her shoulders. She looked up at him, biting her lip. "I cannot, I will surely—"

His words trailed off and he pulled her up next to him as he found his release, clutching her away from his torso, murmuring into her neck. She smiled into his hair, the smell of the tresses she had missed so much that she had not yet washed the pillowcase he had slept on at the Paper Garden.

"Good god," he swore. He looked up at her, his eyes mad and staring. He was panting and he said the two words as if they were the very last in the language to survive. He shimmied the breeches back up his hips and curled against her.

"You are trying to kill me," he sighed.

Ana extracted herself from the embrace and crossed to a full-length mirror. She had held up surprisingly well during the antics. She looked presentable again with just a few pins, lip color, and a handkerchief from her reticule.

"You should probably change, duke," she grinned.

"Harpy. How I have missed you." He got up and hugged her from behind.

"Well, do not leave me again."

"The same goes for you." He kissed her forehead. "But let us not forget that you have a lecture to give. There is a ladies' retiring room two doors from the library, should you require."

"Thoughtful of you." She squeezed his arm. "Will I see you after reading?"

"I will come to the Garden tonight, after I speak with the duchess. I need to tell her that she will be the dowager soon."

"Oh, Eli." A feeling flooded through her that did not have a precedent. It had to be the promise of a better future, she thought. "I cannot believe this is actually happening."

"You must," he said, placing his lips on hers a final time before easing her toward the door. "Now, go preach your sermon. The ladies await your wisdom."

He paused, a giant grin on his face.

"Naughty girl."

She closed the door on his smirk and resisted the urge to skip down the hall.

◆　◆　◆

Elias, the patron saint of hovering in doorways, stood just inside the library. He had changed and come back downstairs, a little calmer. He had a definite sense that he was the luckiest man in the world. His mother scowled when he entered the room, but he crossed his arms and leaned against the wall all the same. It was his home, when it came down to it, and no one could tell him he could not occupy his own library. Not now, not with his beloved Ana standing at a podium, so enchantingly nervous and unsure. He would not miss this.

He tried not to look at her with hunger as she stood there, but he could not help endeavoring to catch her eyes as she shuffled through her papers. Ana spotted him as she rifled and a frown flashed across her face, which only made him smile more. It was evident that she would rather not have him there.

She had a false start and cleared her throat.

"Excuse me, ladies. Thank you once again for having me here. As you all know, I am Analise Quail, the author of the book that you read and discussed. Lady Alessandra has asked me to read some passages, so I shall begin . . ."

She looked down at the paper as she read, but an odd expression appeared on her face when she said the words.

"One should not be treated like a prize stallion when joining hands in marriage. It is no more of an honor to be chosen for one's beauty than to be selected for one's fortune. These are things that tarnish and fade. If true happiness is to be achieved by both parties, it must be founded on a mutual respect and admiration, not just attraction or a business transaction."

Her voice faltered.

"I do apologize. I have never read this aloud to such a large group of people." She fanned herself with one of the sheaves; Elias was astonished to see her unconfident. After a moment, she went on.

"Ahem. The gap between working class women and the nobility is not as deep as we think. It is possible to feel sympathy for the plight of all of our sisters, whether comfortable in estates with cold husbands or shivering in brothels with lechers. Often, these men are one and the same. It is preposterous for us to be chained to these fates, with no way to fulfill ourselves by our own means. Do not think that I say all men are bad men—"

Her eyes darted to him.

"—but some think themselves above reproach."

The rest of the room got a different meaning from the sentence. Elias put his head down so that if any of the ladies turned they would not see his amusement. In his mind, he saw the copy of the book that was still upstairs—those words, meant as a challenge, signed by this impossible woman, using fake initials. The wave of gratitude that she loved him was palpable.

It was then that the room erupted.

"The men will find this insulting!" A voice from the crowd chirped.

Ana only smiled. "Men like to be insulted."

There was a sea of open mouths around him, but when Elias turned to look at his mother, she was nodding in sage agreement.

"This book should be burned," said an older woman with a bitter, pinched face. "It is an uncommon scandal and you will be arrested, Miss Quail."

"It is only sense," Alessandra protested. Once again, Elias felt a swell of pride for his young sister. "Nothing Miss Quail says is harmful to anyone. With a little effort, it can be employed."

"This sort of reform tends to be contagious," a woman lounging on a chaise said. "What is next, Miss Quail, the rights of servants?"

Analise considered. "Well, that would not be a bad thing—"

"It is all nonsense!" Lady Worthington interrupted. "Drastic changes like these will never come about—people are set in their ways. It is the way things work."

"It does not have to be," Alessandra sniffed.

"My daughter is right," the duchess intoned. Alessandra puffed up with pride; she was not used to her mother saying she was correct. "Miss Quail's book is not farfetched. It is reasonable."

Elias was surprised to find that he was in a family of radicals. If Father was still alive, neither Alessandra nor Sophia would have said such things.

"I have a proposition for you, Miss Quail," the duchess went on. "Might you be interested in speaking to a wider circle of ladies? I will sponsor you, of course, and gain entry into fine houses. I would be interested to see the reaction."

"Speaking engagements? With you?" Analise faltered and her eyes flashed to Elias. He tried to telegraph reassurance, but she grew paler and her forehead grew shiny. "My apologies . . . with you, Your Grace?"

"What I am offering, Miss Quail, is my patronage. I know you have not had a London debut and I would agree to usher you into society, lend my respectability, encourage your ideas . . . perhaps we can even find you a suitably high-minded husband."

"I. I, oh, Your Grace—I mean no disrespect . . . but—"

Ana's hands slipped off of the podium and she teetered in a strange way. It was enough to spur Elias to the front of the room. It was good that he did, because by the time he got to her she was on her way to a dead faint. She sank like a sack into his arms and the whole group of ladies gasped. Alessandra shot to her feet.

"Take Miss Quail to my room, Duke," she said, springing into action. "Ladies, I regret that this afternoon will be cut short, but I shall make it up to you at another time."

She barked some orders to maids, for smelling salts and water. Elias was supporting Ana, but she was unconscious. He did not know what had come over her, but it did not matter. Panic coursed through him as he lifted her off her feet. He carried her down the hallway, his mother and sister marching behind him.

◆   ◆   ◆

Ana woke up to the entire family of Lennox hovering in her still-blurry vision.

"Is she waking up?" Alessandra asked, wafting the salts under her nose again. "I think she's waking up."

"Thank the heavens." This, soft, from Elias. He stood a little behind the two women, the worry lines evident in his face.

Ana blinked.

"I fainted," she said.

"Yes," the duchess confirmed in a shocked voice. "In my library! And those ladies likely have it halfway across the city by now!"

She took the glass of water Alessandra handed her, grateful for the coolness. She had fainted. It was the only proper reaction to what the duchess had proposed: accept the patronage of the Lennox family and therefore be something of their pet, shuttled around to society, but held at arm's length. The duchess wanted to marry her off! Her ideas, heard by people in positions of power, but at the expense of Eli's affections. Doomed to watch him from afar for the rest of her life. It was not a choice she could make.

"Whatever came over you?" the duchess asked.

"I am sorry, Your Grace," Ana sat up a bit, ignoring the lingering queasiness. She might as well get the truth out of the way. "I am fine— I simply—I must decline your offer. I must be frank and I shall take all the blame, but . . . I cannot do it. I cannot accept your gracious offer. I am in love with your son."

Elias stepped back, surprise coloring his whole face.

"I cannot bear the silence any longer," she continued, "and I assure you he has not acted in an untoward manner, but it is the reason I cannot fulfill your request. I am flattered and appreciative of your notice, but if I accept your patronage, it will forever divide me from Elias."

The duchess was unruffled. She studied Ana, who resolved not to squirm, but spoke to Eli without turning.

"How long has this been going on, Duke?"

"Months, Mother. It is—she is—the piano player from the gossip pages."

"Ah," the duchess said, putting things together. "I feel that I should have figured that out, really. Well, Lennox? Is this mutual?"

"Very much so."

He smiled at Ana over his mother's head. Her heart expanded, but compressed back as she waited for the imminent verdict from Her Grace.

"Forgive my ignorance of the state of affairs, Miss Quail. But what is the problem here? Are you in some way unsuitable?"

"I am unsuitable in most ways, Your Grace. As you already know, I was employed at a brothel. Though I did not take money for my affections, it is true nonetheless. I am far too outspoken to be a duchess, I suppose, but you are aware of that."

Sophia snorted. "You will find that trait to be useful, I think. What else?"

"My father was a notorious lecher. You may well know him in infamy from your youth in Staffordshire. He was a merchant who petitioned for a peerage and was granted a baronetcy. George Quail."

The duchess's eyebrows pulled together and her mouth turned down fully, marking her as the originator of the facial expression Ana had seen both of her children make.

"Oh, I remember George Quail. A crass man. I did not approve of what he did to your mother, but it was not her fault, nor was it yours. He was a silly thing with no regard for morals or responsibilities. You, my dear, are not a silly thing."

"You may change your mind when we tell you about the Sleeping Dove," Ana smiled with self-deprecation. She had misjudged the duchess, just as she had misjudged her son.

"Nonsense," Sophia sniffed. "I read your book—you are uncommonly sensible. Society will hate you, I'm sure, but things around here needed to be shaken up."

Analise stood. Alessandra helped her, though she did not need it. She felt no trace of faint now that she had endured the conversation she had feared for so long. She removed the sapphire ring from a chain around her neck, the ring that Elias had used as a missile when he thought she had betrayed him.

She held it out to him.

"I brought this, thinking you might demand it back."

Her words hung in the air and it seemed that no one drew a breath. Ana knew that she certainly did not—after the last syllable, she was frozen.

Elias grasped the hand that held the ring, closing her fingertips over it, and dropped to one knee in front of her. Alessandra gasped, her hands shooting to her mouth to stifle a delighted squeak. The duchess's posture was so straight that she was in danger of touching the ceiling with her coiffure.

"We have made a muddle of this, Ana."

"Marvelously," she said, her voice quaking.

"If you do not have any more objections," he grinned up at her, "I would like to ask you to marry me."

Ana's eyes darted to Sophia. She could not gauge the look on her face.

"If your mother cons—"

The duchess waved a hand.

"I said you were not a silly thing; do not prove me wrong." She started out of the room, talking to no one in particular. "I cannot believe we shall have to plan a wedding and honeymoon before the speaking tour. Elias, you have a special talent for making my life difficult. Come now, Alessandra."

"But this is the good part," she complained. She flounced her skirts and followed her mother.

The door shut and Ana gazed down at the man she would spend the rest of her life with, and gladly. He was still smiling. It made him look a touch unhinged.

"I would like to stand up, my lady, and thus I require an answer."

"A resounding yes, Your Grace."

He stood up and placed the ring on her finger, which was much better than hurling it at her, or when it had sat on the shelf. Much more its proper place. Everything seemed in its proper place, as he kissed her in the estate that they would share, her real name in the air, no more secrets to be kept.

"Will things be less adventurous now, Eli?"

"I would think not," he replied, kissing the tip of her nose. "I think they may get even more peculiar."

She smiled.

"Perfect."

EPILOGUE

"I thought we were not going to get involved with this renovation," Analise sighed, dusting her hands off on an apron. "From what I understood, my love, we were going to be silent owners."

Elias put his arms around his wife, sure that his eyes were twinkling in a most absurd manner.

"Do not pretend you are unhappy. You never would have been able to stay at home. If you prefer, we can leave poor Sally to do all of this on her own."

"Don't you dare!" Sally said, setting down a tray of glasses. Nicholas was behind her in an instant, ready with an affectionate pinch. He had taken to doing that a lot. Elias could see now why Nicholas had agreed so quickly to the proposition of buying the Sleeping Dove—it was a convenient way to keep Sally in his life. Even if he did not yet realize it, Nicholas was delaying his search for a wife and integrating Miss Hopewell into his daily life.

Elias smiled, something that he could not seem to stop doing these days. He looked around the room—the velvet of the gambling tables had replaced the worn tops of oak where Eli's restless leg had once bounced, before he had known Ana. The light was warm amber instead of a dim void. The new sign out front read The Weeping Martyr, which amused him to no end. All and all, there was no longer a look of hopelessness. It was as if the renovation of the courtyard seeped into the rest of the building. The only thing that remained the same was the piano.

He took her hand and led her to it.

"Play me a tune, Your Grace?"

Ana groaned.

"When will you get tired of that?"

She fell into his lap when he pulled her onto the bench.

"Never. It annoys you so prettily."

She started playing in an absent manner, because he was kissing her neck.

"We must go to the Spencers' ball tonight," he muttered into her skin. "Cannot be avoided."

Ana issued yet another growl. "You, sir, do not have the same experience as I at these balls. You will just disappear with Frost and leave me to answer a barrage of questions from chirping gossips."

"Hmm?" Frost said, popping up from under the bar at the mention of his name. "Before I forget, someone remind me to put some of the special sherry out here."

Elias ignored him and kissed his wife's neck again. "But the society ladies like you so much more than me, Duchess."

He took up the keys with her, as he had when they first met. Now everything about their lives had become a duet.

"You were supposed to make my life less complicated, Duke," she said pointedly. "Now I run a gambling hall, attend to society, and am toted around with your mother to speak to often-disgruntled circles of women who disagree with my book. Good show."

"I do not think I ever promised that," he mused. There was a crash from the other side of the room and Thackeray cursed. "Indeed, I cannot promise that."

He looked on top of the piano. The morning paper was there, as always, and Ana had it open to a Cruikshank illustration. Elias always secretly wished to have one of his own, and he was more than happy with the outcome: him, caught in a net, the end of it held by the new duchess. The Uncatchable, caught.

He could give a damn what others thought. The Duke of Lennox was happy to be well and truly caught.

ACKNOWLEDGMENTS

Winning an Amazon Breakthrough Novel Award is a very strange experience. But, as you have this book in your hand now, I would like to thank the people who helped make that happen.

My team at Amazon has been stellar, especially Terry Goodman, Thom Kephart, Alison Dasho, and the amazing ladies of Montlake Romance (Hai-Yen Mura, Susan Stockman, Jessica Poore, JoVon Sotak, Kelli Martin, and Maria Gomez). My developmental editor, Jenna Free, is a true gem. She really understood the book and then helped me make it even better. I know this thing must have been a beast to copyedit, so my thanks also go to the brave Cassie Armstrong.

My family is truly outstanding. My gram and my mother spent countless hours reading to me when I was a little girl. Hearing my gram and pap giggle on the phone when they found out about ABNA was one of the best parts of this experience. Mom, Dad, and Justin: thank you for keeping the secret and for allowing me to grow up with my imagination intact. The three Ross aunts, Debbie, Ellen, and Kathy, have all been instrumental influences and sources of strength.

My friends who have supported and counseled me through creative work: Al Dorantes, Kelly Pressler, Anne DeHart, Joe Baumiller, Jason Gloeckl, Anthony Vesci, Ashly Nagrant, James Foreman, and dozens of important others. Amy Loveridge, there is no way to thank you for what you have done. I hope my eternal gratitude is enough. Jocelyn Hillen: honeydude, I love you. If it weren't for you, I might have quit long ago.

My writing partners and couchmates are my husband, Steve, and our cats, Orson and Ro. I simply could not do this without you.

ABOUT THE AUTHOR

Evelyn Pryce lives in Pittsburgh, where she founded a charity organization that raises money for literacy and supports artists. In her spare time, she reads, blogs, gardens, and attempts to cook. In the past, she has written comic books and fronted rock bands. She is not as domesticated as she sounds. She would love to connect with readers at evelynpryce.com.